Ex-Boyfriend on Aisle 6

Ex-Boyfriend
on Aisle 6

STORIES BY

Susan Jackson Rodgers

Press 53
Winston-Salem

Press 53, LLC
PO Box 30314
Winston-Salem, NC 27130

First Edition

Cover design by Alyssa Hughes and Martha J. Baker

Cover art, "Shopping Cart," Copyright © 2012
by Colby Johnson, used by permission of the artist.
www.lazydayphoto.com

Author photo by Hannah McIntosh

Printed on acid-free paper
ISBN 978-1-935708-65-0

LRR

Versions of the following stories appeared in these publications:

"Fiona in the Vortex" (*Beloit Fiction Journal*), "Ex-Boyfriend on Aisle 6" (*Third Wednesday*), "This Other Alan" and "Chicken Man" (*North American Review*), "Thirty" (*Midwestern Gothic*), "What Happens Next" (*Prairie Schooner*), "That Reminds Me" (*Quick Fiction*), "Anniversary" (*Blue Mesa Review*), "Bodies" (as "Outside" in *New England Review*), "I've Looked Everywhere" (*StoryQuarterly*; reprinted in the anthology *Voices in Today's Magazines*, Long Ridge Writers Group), "This Day" (*Glimmer Train*), "Where Are They Now?" (in the anthology *Keeping Track: Fiction of Lists*, Main Street Rag Press).

Ex-Boyfriend on Aisle 6

Fiona in the Vortex

I agreed to water my former neighbor's plants while she was out of town, even though her husband had died and I was nervous about going into her house alone. I thought the ghost of this husband might be hanging around, waiting for me to show up. He might be miffed that I had neglected his wife in recent years. She and I had once been friends, but we drifted apart after my own marriage. When I lived next door to Fiona, I wasn't married. I was convinced I would always be alone. This fear occasionally led me to test out my powers of attraction. I'm ashamed to say that I tested my powers on the dead husband—well, he wasn't dead yet. I gardened in my bathing suit, bending over to weed, my backside facing Fiona's kitchen window. I stretched languorously, in such obvious ways I often embarrassed myself and went inside. Fiona, fifteen years older than I was, had always been kind to me; I even felt strangely protective towards her. Yet there I was trying to lure Max, her husband— to do what? I didn't even know.

Then I met my husband. I sold my house, and we bought a new, larger house on the other side of town. I became pregnant with twins almost immediately, boys, and when they were two, I had a daughter, and another year later, a son. My husband agreed to a vasectomy.

Of course my new responsibilities exhausted me.

But I should've made time for Fiona. I often felt guilty about her. She was dependent upon Max, and his death must have exacerbated her problems. She hated driving, and suffered from obsessive-compulsive tendencies. She had to keep checking things, the lights, the appliances, the locked door, the answering machine. She stared at the light bulb in the kitchen, watching the light go off when she flicked the switch, but still stared and stared—was the light off? Or did it just *look* as if it were off? How could she be sure? Even turning the light on again, then off, didn't help, and when I lived next door I often watched her nightly routine with an acute sense of anticipation, the lights in each room going on, then off, then on; I held my breath waiting to see how long it would take for the whole house to go dark. She hadn't always been like this. She seemed almost normal when I first moved in.

In the mornings before I left for work—Max put in long shifts at a bakery he managed, and was gone at 3 a.m.—I'd check on her, bring in the newspaper, share the news I'd heard while doing my treadmill. She liked human interest pieces, but no hard news or politics, nothing too remote (war, famine, polar ice caps). She liked the stories about people who keep their deceased family members in the house: skeletons lounging in basement recliners, calcified remains in the guest room bed. She couldn't get enough of the interviews with neighbors. "We hadn't seen Mrs. So-and-So for a few months, but we just figured she was on vacation."

Max died one morning, cardiac arrest, at work. At his funeral, Fiona embraced me for a long time. "He thought the world of you," she said weepily into my ear. Then she gave me a quick kiss on the lips. We were both startled. She hadn't meant to do it.

When she asked me about the plants, we hadn't spoken in six months, maybe longer. I saw her in the freezer section of the grocery store. I had the baby with me; the twins were in kindergarten and my daughter in preschool. Fiona wasn't exactly muttering to herself, but close. I approached carefully. "Hi Fiona." She looked up, her face crinkling with recognition. She was wearing her black hair in a braid coiled on top of her head, and had made an effort to apply eye shadow, lipstick, blush. We chatted for a few minutes. She never once acknowledged the baby, though I saw her taking sidelong glances, as if at any moment he might rise up on plump elbows and spit venom. She told me about her recent activities, mall walking and a laughter therapy group, as well as a new treatment that seemed to be helping. "EFT," she said, as if everyone had heard of it, as if she had said *Lacrosse* or *Fruit Loops*. She demonstrated, tapping herself on her head and face and wrists while saying her affirmations loudly in front of the Lean Cuisines: *I am whole, I am safe, I am sound; I am whole, I am safe . . .* tapping, tapping, tapping. Emotional Freedom Technique, it was called. The baby, understandably, started crying.

I wasn't eager to renew the friendship, but when she asked if I could take care of the plants while she went on a shamanic retreat, it seemed like the least I could do.

I went to her house to receive keys and instructions. It was a Saturday afternoon, so I left the children with my husband. I didn't want them at Fiona's; I remembered her shelves of miniature urns and pots and figurines, and I could easily imagine the destruction if my twins were let loose. But when I got there, I discovered that the tchotchkes had been put away. Her living room looked neutral now, beige and calm, like a waiting room: couch and several chairs around a coffee table, with three old magazines—*National Geographic, Crochet World, Elle*—neatly fanned on top. The covers asked impossible questions. *Exploration: Where do we go next? Starter marriage: Is yours set to expire?*

"You've redecorated, Fiona," I said.

"Yes," she smiled. "The clutter was causing problems." She

waved her hand around, a vague gesture that referred, apparently, to various channels or pathways or other invisible conduits.

Fiona had made tea, and remembered that I only liked mine iced. She always bought excellent teas from a specialty store. She checked the stove three times to be sure it was off—the "hot surface" warning light could, I agreed, be confusing. She showed me the plants in question. She would be gone for a month, and they needed water twice a week, Mondays and Thursdays. We talked briefly about Max, and hearing his name again made me blush—I'm a redhead, I blush easily—but Fiona didn't seem to notice. She gave me a house key and elaborate instructions about how to open the door, which she said had a tendency to stick.

"I'm so glad you're able to make this trip," I said.

Fiona nodded. "Me too. I look forward to continuing the healing process."

I drove slowly home, glad to have the time in the car by myself, no radio, no CD. It was spring, finally, after a bitter Midwestern winter, and I rolled down the windows and relished the balminess of the air. I felt that sudden rush of gratitude for my life, for all the good things in it, and felt sad for Fiona, Fiona alone on her mythical quest, Fiona attempting to harness the spiritual energies of the universe. At home I was met with the usual madness, the twins fighting over a truck in the sandbox in the backyard (even though there were two identical trucks available, *that one*, they both insisted, was the best). My daughter had managed to get the flour out of the kitchen cabinet as well as every mixing bowl, and was having a fine time with that project, which included water, food coloring, and Karo syrup. My husband was feeding the baby in the dining room, oblivious to the chaos surrounding him, or perhaps enjoying it.

I made a hasty note on my kitchen calendar, and didn't think about Fiona again until Monday arrived. "F.? Water?" I murmured. These notes often feel like clues that someone else has left behind for me, breadcrumbs in the forest. My husband decoded the message, then handed me a fussing baby and kissed me on the back of my neck. He was in charge of getting the twins to school and our daughter to preschool, and jovially loaded everybody into the car, as if he were the visiting uncle having a fine time and not the parent who did this every day. I had until noon, when I picked up the preschooler, to accomplish a myriad of domestic tasks. The tasks would suck up the day, like a good vacuum cleaner. I figured I'd better go to Fiona's first.

Fiona was right. The door did stick. I finally managed to get it open on the fifth try, the baby in his carrier on the stoop, watching me with his usual bemusement. I called out, "Hello? Anybody home?" just in case. Maybe Fiona didn't make it to Sedona after all. My own voice in the house, calling out, made me nervous, and I was glad to have the baby with me as a kind of buffer or shield, someone to talk to. "See, this is Fiona's house, and Mommy used to live in that white house with the green shutters. I had a pretty little garden behind the picket fence, with all kinds of flowers—alyssum, and larkspur, and sweet William." He smiled at me, hearing his name. "Yes, you're William too, aren't you?" I missed that garden, the bright blooms, the satisfaction of arranging the world to my liking, the pleasures of digging around in the dirt.

The living room was as I remembered. Magazines on the coffee table, chairs clustered eagerly around. I put the baby's carrier on the floor. A single shaft of light shone through half-closed blinds; dust motes floated in this beam, and for a moment we were both transfixed. It was so quiet! I waved my fingers through the motes and William laughed. I gave him my keys to play with while I watered the plants in the kitchen, using the red plastic watering can Fiona had left on the counter. When I was done, I stood at the kitchen sink. There was my old garden, and, I imagined, the ghostly image of my former self, leaning over in short-shorts—oh, I had looked good back then. I smiled, watching. My old self was wearing a floppy white canvas hat that I hadn't thought of until this minute. Where had that hat gone? I remembered the hat, and remembered the exact spot I used to hang it, on a hook inside the door, where I also hung a sky blue cardigan and a barn jacket and an umbrella. If I walked into that house now, I thought, the hat would still be there, and perhaps other things I had lost track of—a painted dish from Russia, where I kept stray buttons and safety pins; a polished stone paper weight; a scatter rug I bought at an arts fair, with blues and purples and greens—I loved that little rug. Where was it? Thrown away or given away, I couldn't recall. I reached my hand out toward the house and the self as if I could touch them.

My thinner younger self straightened, and stood with her hands on her hips, peering in my direction. She had sensed someone watching her, getting an eyeful of that sweet derriere. She took a step forward—the glare on Fiona's window would make it difficult to see. I stepped aside. I waited until she went away.

I had the terrible feeling that I would return to the living room, and the baby would be gone. I often had these irrational fears about the children. After all, they had not even existed until recently. We felt powerful, my husband and I. We had made people where people had not been before! Rabbits from hats! Reproduction seemed like a pretty impressive trick. But now that the children were here, we had a lot to keep track of.

I rushed back to the living room. William was there, of course, asleep now, my keys in his fist. Sometimes he had the look of his older self: I could see the little boy he was about to become. But when sleeping, he was all baby, and I couldn't picture him ever growing older, walking, talking, going to school like my other children. I sat on the couch—I didn't want to take the keys from him and risk waking him up. The couch fabric was a nubby dark green and brown, foresty and dense. I leaned back and closed my eyes. Of course, I fell asleep. When I woke up, it was late—I had only five minutes to get to the preschool. The baby jolted and cried when I moved him into the car. He cried for a long time.

Fiona called me that night. "How is everything there?" she asked. We talked for a while. She was disappointed in her progress so far, but determined to stay open minded. She had hiked to the upflow vortex at Airport Mesa, and found some fellow pilgrims who told her to try Boynton Canyon, the most powerful vortex in Sedona. I imagined a whirling around, Dorothy in the tornado, but she said it wasn't like that. "I'm going to a Medicine Wheel ceremony tomorrow," she added. "Did you remember to turn off my lights?" I assured her I had, but I couldn't remember if I had turned them off or not. I couldn't remember if I turned them on in the first place. An image of my young self, standing in her living room, looking at Fiona's house, came unbidden. That self was just waiting for those lights to go off once and for all so she could go to bed.

"You aren't really going back over there now?" my husband asked. He was sitting on the couch, sweating from his evening run. His sweat would stain the fabric of the couch. I tapped him lightly on the shoulder, hoping he would get the hint, but he interpreted my gesture in the opposite way and leaned back, his soaked shirt pressed against the couch cushions. I made a mental note to Febreze later.

"I won't be able to sleep."

"Aren't you afraid of Max the Ghost?"

"Ha ha. The twins need a bath, please. The baby is already down. Natalie is listening to her tape in bed."

He removed his big shoes and peeled off the sweaty socks. He had lovely strong feet, but one of his toenails was turning black from all the training. He examined the toenail with visible pride.

"Call me if you hear any scary noises."

I left him admiring his trophy toe. Fiona's house, as it turned out, was dark. But my old house was lit up. Every room in it. I idled at the curb for a few minutes, then turned off the engine, waiting to see if I could glimpse the inhabitants. No one appeared to be home. No car in the driveway, the garage door closed. I rolled down my window. The air smelled like rain. A breeze lifted up.

I stepped out of the car. My plan was just to walk around the block. I hadn't been back to the old neighborhood at night, and walking up the sidewalk gave me that strange disconnected feeling. Did I still live here? Had I dreamed all that other life? That husband, those children? I stood near the lilac trees that bordered my old backyard. The world smelled of early spring. I put one hand on the picket fence I had painted. I remembered the day, the paint, the brush, the sunburn on my arms, the guy I had been dating at the time, the music we listened to, the job I liked at first and then hated. I remembered other things too. I planted the tulip bulbs *there*. The boyfriend broke up with me *there*. I lay in the sun peeking over at Max *there*. I buried my cat *there*. I nearly burned down the detached garage by lighting my hibachi *there*.

I lifted the latch on the gate and strolled into my old backyard. Fiona's house looked at me expectantly, its empty window boxes reminding me of fanny packs, or tool belts: Max had always used the window boxes to store trash bags, grass seed, wrenches. I sat on my old back stoop. When I sat here before, in my old life, I often drank a beer. I smoked clove cigarettes. I listened to Bonnie Raitt. I thought my life had stalled out and I would never figure out how to get it started again. I made regrettable late night phone calls to old boyfriends. I waved my arms when I talked, and laughed too loudly at parties. I cooked big dinners and invited people over and made pitchers of strong drinks— martinis, margaritas, mojitos. I wore a canvas hat and a bikini in my garden. I kissed Max.

I gasped, as if I hadn't actually remembered kissing him until now.

But I did kiss him. Once. *There*, behind the garage I almost burned down. He was taking out his trash. I was struggling to get my lawn mower into the garage, which was barely big enough to hold my car, let alone yard paraphernalia. Max came over to help. He was bald, with glasses and a paunch, but his face was kind, even handsome—you could tell he'd been cute in his youth. He still had the twinkling eyes of a player. It was my idea, the kiss. Not even an idea. Impulse. I was swept up by the energy. I was flirting, shaking his hand playfully to thank him for his help, then a peck on the cheek, except I didn't move away, and neither did he. He made a little sound in his throat. I thought it was something in the garage rafters at first—a bird or mouse. He made a sound then turned his head almost imperceptibly, but not imperceptibly, I *perceived* the turn and turned too and then of course we were kissing. Not just a peck either. An involved and complex kiss that frankly makes me a little weak-kneed to recall, even now. Oh, he was a good kisser, that Max. He knew what he was doing. And he smelled delicious, pumpernickel and brandy. We stepped delicately apart, flushed and breathless.

"Melanie," he finally said. He smiled. "I won't say I'm sorry."

I smiled back. "Me neither."

We were saying, But this won't happen again.

He walked back to his house. I smoked my clove cigarette on the stoop, waiting around to see if anything else would happen.

Fiona's lights went off. Then on again. And off. And so forth.

Now I found my spare backdoor key under a rock, right where I had left it all those years ago. I had this vague notion that I might go into my old house and take a look around. I could see so clearly all the things I'd left behind. I stood up, key in hand.

Then I heard laughter—a man's. Sudden laughing, followed by silence. The laughing came from inside my old house, or from another house nearby with a window open, or maybe it was leftover from when Max lived here. It did sound like Max. I put the key in my pocket, and walked back to my car. The rain started shortly after I got home.

Fiona called the next day with good news. She'd had a breakthrough! She left a high-pitched, manic message on the machine. "I'm staying on," she said. She could feel the seismic shifts, the tectonic plates of her soul, she went on like that with many beautiful geologic metaphors.

Outside the grocery store that afternoon, flats of pansies were for sale. I decided to plant some in Fiona's window boxes. The empty boxes had always bothered me. Whoever lived in my old house could enjoy these pansies from her kitchen window. I examined the pansy faces; how fierce they looked, like mad Muppets or orangutans, scowling. Their frilly manes ruffled in the breeze. I picked out a flat of purple flowers with benign expressions, flowers who looked at the world with equanimity. In Fiona's kitchen, I put the kettle on to boil, made myself a pot of her good tea, and poured it in a pitcher with ice. I dumped new potting soil in the window boxes, planted the flowers, and watered them with the red watering can. I sat for a few minutes on Fiona's front stoop, drinking my tea. I closed my eyes.

Across the way, my old self stepped out her front door and lifted her face to the sunshine. She was dressed up, wearing a flowery skirt I loved, yellow poppies on a black background. The skirt, I recalled, had a zipper on the side, and was made of rayon, or some other floaty material, dry clean only. The young woman looked fresh and young and pleased with herself. She didn't notice the pansies, or me. She was full of purpose, a feeling I'd forgotten she had. Good for her, I thought. Maybe she knows where she's going after all. She strode down the street, a straw bag over her freckled shoulder, chin lifted. She swayed as she walked, and I remembered the deliberate wag of the hips, the self-conscious, important feeling that someone was indeed watching. She turned the corner without looking back.

I dug the old key out of my jeans pocket. I buried it in the wet window-box dirt. Then I went inside, to check the stove.

Ex-Boyfriend on Aisle 6

If they could just warn you. Like when a kid pushes his mother's cart into the pickle jars, and the strained managerial voice reverberates through the store: *Clean up on aisle 6.* If you could have that kind of system in place. *Ex-boyfriend on aisle 6. And, um, watch out because he's with—well, someone a lot younger than you.* But no. Instead it's you with your out-of-control cart, or so it seems, as you go careening around a corner and head straight into—shit, shit, shit. It's midnight for God's sake. It's midnight, the kids are at their father's this weekend, and normally you wouldn't even be out this late but you don't sleep well when the children aren't home, and you figured you might as well use this time to pick up a few groceries. You've tried everything else. The treadmill, the yoga DVD, three vodka tonics, a movie on TV in which the mother is about to die and a much younger woman is about to marry the ex-husband and, therefore, become the mother of the dying mother's children. So on top of the sweating and the drinking, you've also been (another Saturday night! Hurray!) sobbing uncontrollably.

Oh, you look swell all right.

And of course it's too late—he's spotted you. So even if

you could pretend—*on second thought I don't need anything down this aisle after all*—it's too late because he's seen you and so has the giggly girl, who has one hand on a bag of Ranch Doritos, and the other in the ex-boyfriend's back jeans pocket. You know exactly what a hand in that pocket feels like.

If only you had, for instance, showered.

If only you had changed out of the workout capris that you once thought were cute but that (you now know) actually make your butt look baggy, fallen, a fallen butt. If you had washed your face even, or better yet your hair. If you'd put on some goddamn make-up—a swipe of lipstick, a dab of concealer. But who shops at midnight, except drunks and people on the 3-11 shift and people who don't want to see anybody? Who knew he'd be here? Who knew he'd be with that shiny-haired, perfect-complexioned, high-butted creature? *Ex-boyfriend on aisle 6!* Someone could have warned you. *Emotional melt-down on aisle 6! Humiliation! Mortification! Watch out for that—you're about to step right into—*

"Hi," he says. The smile is predictably apologetic but not really, really he's faking, he's coy as if he's hiding something behind his back and you have already caught a glimpse of it. Which is exactly what has happened.

"Oh, hi." He knows what the "oh" means. The "oh" is hesitation, also fake, and he knows you are horrified by how you look, how you feel, how you are. Everything that's happened rises up in an instant between you: his role in your divorce, your pending child custody battle, your rapid descent into what feels a lot like poverty. It's all his fault. Well, and yours. And yours. Of course. And that's what the "oh"—flimsy shield—protects you against. Oh—it's you. Oh—I don't care. Oh—I see you've moved on. Oh—oh—oh—I'm a fucking idiot.

He's about to introduce you to the tanned, belly-button-pierced midriff standing next to him. But you just keep pushing the cart. There's no dignity in walking away, or in ignoring her theatrical disbelief (that girlish gasp and giggle). Nothing has been saved here. You just get to push your cart to aisle 7. And the first impulse? To abandon the cart, and race, baggy butt and all, for the exit? No. Because you need the things in the cart. The limes. The coffee. The king-sized generic Ibuprofen, the bar of dark chocolate, the bag of ice, the *Entertainment Weekly*, the Lean Cuisines, the tonic, the B-complex vitamins.

They're ahead of you now anyway—they're having a good time at the self-checkout, feeding bills into the slot and laughing. You realize now they're stoned. By the time you get to the cashier, they've slipped away with their snacks and their hands on each other, and if he's thinking of you at all, it's as a girl he once slept with, it's as evidence to the current girl that he gets around.

Manny, the checkout guy's nametag reads. Manny has pimples and a soul patch. "Manny," you confide as he slides your items along the scanner. Manny appears to be stoned as well. Is everyone stoned? Why don't they share? "A bit of a mess on aisle 6, Manny. You'll need a bucket and a mop and a big jug of Pine-Sol." He nods, sighs, takes your money. You have just enough time to hear his ragged voice on the speaker as you push your cart into the night.

This Other Alan

The houses in Leah's dreams were always poorly constructed, with dark tunnels instead of hallways, and trapdoors she had to heave herself through to reach the second floor. The rooms were filled with unlikely collectibles—saltshakers in one, peacock feathers in another. Entrances involved ladders, or hopping from one unstable rock to another. One house had three kitchens and a bayonet room. Another had no bathroom. Sometimes the houses were patched-together composites of places she had once lived, or visited. Other times they were alien to her. She drifted from house to house, confused, restless. The houses were so impractical! Who would live here? How would you get your groceries from this garage (which was on stilts) to the entryway, several floors below? Would you fly? Was there a pulley system? She woke up relieved to be in her own house, which was cluttered but navigable.

She knew what Jung would say about dream houses representing the psyche. Leah was building her inner self. But wasn't she done with that project yet? She was well past forty. The inner self's construction should be complete by now.

The night she attended a new friend's dinner party, she felt she had dreamed the house before, although it was quite ordinary—no tunnels or pulleys or (visible) trapdoors. The friend's name was Therese Grimbault. They had met in yoga class, where they were assigned as partners to practice headstands. Therese, upside down and red-faced, had introduced herself in her French Canadian accent—*by the way, Yoga Partner, my name is Therese*—and this struck Leah as funny. She held on to Therese's ankles but to no avail; Therese collapsed, both of them lost in a fit of laughter. "Church giggles," Therese said in the parking lot afterwards. Leah suggested a glass of wine, and Therese made an "of course" gesture, as if wine went without saying. Leah followed Therese to a tapas bar on Washington Street in Somerville, where Therese lived, and sangria became part of the yoga routine.

Therese spoke openly about her life, her second marriage to a man named Alan, her past as a model in Toronto, her fear of accidental death, her concerns about her diminishing libido. Leah was drawn to women like this, who instantly offered up intimate details that were none of Leah's or anyone else's business. Leah herself was more reticent, "reserved," her late husband once said, though she didn't feel that way—reserved sounded stuffy, and Leah thought of herself as warm and open. But maybe she was not. Maybe she was like her houses, dream and otherwise, cluttered, unwieldy, unnecessarily complicated. In any case, Therese sensed in Leah a willing recipient of information, and that was how Leah knew about, for instance, Therese and Alan's penchant for sex in almost-public places, when they were first dating. Leah told Therese very little.

Leah had once dated a man named Alan. They lived together in Maine after college. She hadn't thought about him much, until meeting Therese and hearing about *her* Alan. Therese's Alan played racquetball, listened to hip hop, cooked elaborate egg white omelets, and emailed ex-girlfriends in an attempt, he said, to reconnect with his past. This Alan sounded nothing like Leah's Alan. So she was surprised to discover, the night of Therese's party, that the two Alans were in fact one and the same. Indeed, Alan Walker—the Alan she had loved all those years ago—greeted her now at the door.

"Leah! Wow. I had no idea—"

"Therese said she was married to Alan. I never thought it was you." They laughed, embraced, exclaimed. She met again his good woodsy smell, slightly smoky and herbish. She recalled some other things too.

"So is it still Leah Fulton?"

"Still is. Though I was married, for a time." She didn't say she was widowed. People always assumed divorce, and that was easier to sidestep in conversation. Death, on the other hand, had to be dealt with.

She took off her red wool coat and gave it to Alan Walker, who hung it on one of the hooks behind him. Hooks for coats, boots lined up underneath a white bench. His curly hair was just as Leah remembered, except for the touches of gray. His eyes held the same combination of melancholy and merriment that drew her to him the first time.

"It's been—what—twenty years?"

"Twenty-four," Leah said. She thought of Alan dancing to hip-hop in his boxers, googling ex-girlfriends. Why hadn't he emailed *her*?

"Though maybe let's not reminisce now, if that's okay? Therese . . . she tends to be a little . . ." Leah nodded. Therese liked drama. "I'll just tell her at the right time," Alan assured her.

Leah wondered when the right time would be, and which part of their life together he would pass on. Maybe he would describe the apartment he and Leah had shared on High Street in Portland for six months. Or maybe he would edit out the living together part. He'd say the apartment was Leah's, and he just spent a lot of time there, which was not so far from the truth. The apartment—a studio, too small for two people—*was* Leah's. He moved in after his own lease ran out. Oh, she hadn't thought of that place for a while. That apartment had not appeared in her nightly real estate adventures. Would he tell Therese about the rat they found in the bedroom, or the smell of Vietnamese food from the apartment next door, or the homeless man who rummaged through their trash—how Alan regularly dropped boxes of crackers and cans of tuna from their fire escape? The man always looked up, bewildered, as if tuna cans were raining down from the sky.

Maybe he would tell the story about how Leah locked them out of the apartment on Labor Day. They couldn't reach the landlady (no cell phones or cyber cafes back then) and wandered downtown with the last of the summer tourists, stopping at pay phones every hour. Leah had looked forward to their one day off, and here they were stuck pacing the harbor. They both had terrible jobs. Alan was a waiter at a family-style seafood place, Leah a secretary for a contractor who turned out to be crooked. But the day turned out all right. They ate slices of pizza and ice cream cones. They went to a music store and Alan played guitar for her, which she hadn't known he could do, a dream already discarded at twenty-two. At dusk they walked through a neighborhood and looked at the houses, the lives inside the rooms, and picked out where they would live if they could. They finally gave up on the landlord, and broke in to the apartment with alarming ease.

Leah had liked being with Alan Walker. When he left her to go back to Boston for graduate school, she was sad for a long time. She couldn't recall, now, why she had not gone with him. Perhaps he had not asked her to.

"Leah! Finally!" Therese called, though Leah was not late. Therese wore a long black dress with slits up both sides and no shoes, toenails painted purple like a teenager's, her fair hair swept up messily, a large silver pendant on a chain around her neck. "You two have met, I see," she said in her singsong way. She took Leah by the elbow and guided her into the living room. "Watch that step there," Therese said, then almost tripped on her own dress. The house again felt familiar to Leah. Had she been here before? In a dream, or perhaps years ago at someone else's party? She knew (as Therese introduced her to the architect, the lawyer, the bookstore owner, the high school teacher, the social worker—Therese seemed to have something for everyone) what would come next: over to the right, a sitting room with a fireplace; straight ahead a hallway to the kitchen; a curving staircase that led to a landing; upstairs, three bedrooms clustered around a bathroom with a clawfoot tub and pedestal sink.

Therese delivered Leah back to the kitchen, where Alan Walker was in charge of cocktails.

"I've been here before," she said. Alan mixed her a vodka martini. She could see he misunderstood—thought she meant, *in this situation before, meeting up with an ex-lover unexpectedly.* She rushed to clarify. "In this house, I mean. Not déjà vu. I've actually been here."

"We've only lived here a year. We were in Woburn, but Therese wanted to be closer to work. We bought the house from Mel and Evelyn Morrison. Do you know them?"

But the Morrisons did not ring a bell. Maybe it was the people before that. Leah shrugged. Here was Alan Walker offering her a drink. Therese laughed her loud laugh in the next room. Leah refused to exchange looks with her old boyfriend, to make any comment, nonverbal or otherwise, about Therese's laughter, which sometimes sounded phony. She and Alan drifted to the hors d'oeuvres table. She didn't know anyone else at the party. She wasn't supposed to even know Alan. She nibbled at a triangle of toasted pita bread.

"So? Kids? Work? Hobbies? What's your life like?"

"My life," she said, smiling, "my life is good. I work for an agency that funds environmental programs. I do public relations, mostly. My son is in graduate school. I'm single at the moment. Which is fine. I mean, I like being alone." She took another bite of pita, felt herself flush. "How about you?"

Alan Walker kept the knowing irony out of his face and

voice, which she appreciated. It would've been easy to flirt, to engage in a dance of double-entendres. She wanted him to, and was also glad he did not. He told her his story. He had finished his degree at Boston Architectural College, then worked for a firm designing grocery stores and megachurches. He quit and began a consulting business. Leah wondered what "consulting" meant. She always thought that Alan had some family money, though he had never told her the details; maybe he didn't need to consult much. Therese was his second wife. He had two daughters from his first marriage. He didn't get to see them as much as he liked, he said, as they lived in North Carolina with their mother. One was fourteen, one sixteen. "Divorce is tough on the kids," he said. "As you know."

She shook her head. "Actually, my husband died. My son was only five, and doesn't remember much about him." She put up her hand, warding off his apologies. "It was a long time ago."

"And you never remarried?"

"Almost. Twice, in fact. But no."

"There's still time."

"Yes."

They had been young together a lifetime ago, and now here they were, these altered selves, hair gray at the temples, lines around the same old mouths and eyes. She was reminded of that TV crime show where two actors portrayed a single character: the young version who had committed a crime years or even decades before, and the older version whom the police had finally tracked down to resolve the "cold" case. At the end of the show, the young version walked past the detective in handcuffs; the detective looked grimly satisfied; the camera returned to the criminal, except now he was his older self again, his present self. This was how it felt to talk to Alan. If she looked away, her mind conjured up the twenty-two-year-old Alan, thinner face, more hair, lankier build. And then she looked back at him, and here he was. This other Alan.

If he weren't married to Therese, and the two of them met at a party, they would go home together.

"It's so good to see you again," Leah said. She didn't mean "good." She meant "disruptive." She shook her head, excused herself to find the bathroom. He started to direct her, but she knew where it was. Therese was shooing people toward the dining room where a buffet was laid out. "Food's getting cold!" she warned. Leah waved at her. The stairs were carpeted, and halfway up there was the landing and a window from which Leah could see the backyard, lit by a streetlight. She climbed the stairs as if she were in one of her dreams, except there were stairs instead of a ladder or a rope she had to shimmy up. She stepped into each room, flicking on the light switch. She had remembered the master bedroom correctly, and the bathroom with the clawfoot tub, but the other bedrooms she had confused with some other house. One was a guest room. The other was Alan's office. Pictures of his daughters sat on the bookshelves. He was right. They were beautiful. An acoustic guitar stood on a stand, pages of music scattered on the floor nearby. Good for him, she thought.

At one time, Leah assumed she and her husband would live in a house like this, with its art on the walls, its comfortable and stylish furniture. They were married only six years when he died. They had spent those years living in a shabby rental in Watertown, waiting for better times.

Leah went into the bathroom, washed her hands, dampened her flushed cheeks. Her eyes were bright. As a general principle she tried not to dwell on the past. She found a brush in a basket on one of the shelves and ran it through her dark hair. Her husband had been depressed. He had wandered aimlessly in the rooms of his own inner house, day after day, unable to find his way out. She had not been able to help him. He died of heartbreak, his mother used to say, but that wasn't true. He died by putting a gun to his head.

She had put it all aside. She had raised their son Zach. She took him to Cub Scout meetings and baseball practice. She fixed him dinners, attended parent-teacher conferences, made a home for him. Sometimes she worried he was like his father.

When Leah stepped into the hallway and saw the linen closet, she remembered: She had been in this house with Zach. He had come to a birthday party here. The children played hide-and-go-seek. When Leah arrived to pick him up, the house was full of children and parents and party chaos. Zach was still hiding. Leah walked through the rooms, calling him, telling him it was time to go. Finally she opened the linen closet door, as she did now, as if Zach might still be there. The closet had a recessed area and he had crawled into a corner. He was balled up and wouldn't come out. "I want to stay here," he said. "I like it here." She got inside the closet with him, coaxing, insisting, but he was stubborn and wouldn't budge. She sat with him for five minutes, ten. His father had been dead three months to the day. The smell of wool and talcum powder engulfed them. It was possible they fell asleep.

She didn't remember what happened next. Eventually, she must have persuaded Zach to leave. There was some embarrassment as they came down the stairs—the parents of the birthday boy were in the middle of a post-party tiff, and hadn't realized that Leah and Zach were still in the house. She walked down those same stairs now, remembering. The angry wife and husband stood right there, next to the couch. They were arguing about who should clean up. A guest had spilled juice on the carpet (Leah imagined she could still see the faint stain, though the carpeting had been replaced). The woman—Leah couldn't even remember her name—held a rag and a bottle of rug cleaner. She was exhausted, she said. "I don't know how much more of this I can take." Zach held Leah's hand as they stood on the landing, waiting to be noticed, not wanting to interrupt. "Maybe we're invisible," Zach whispered. She felt that way too. No one could really see her. No one wanted to. She was the suicide's wife. What do you say to such a person?

The arguing couple had turned, startled. "Leah!" the wife exclaimed. "What on earth are you still doing here?"

She felt that shame now, in Alan Walker's house. *What on earth are you still doing here?*

Leah filled her plate at Therese's table. She found a seat on the couch and ate grilled vegetables, tandoori chicken, salad. Next to her was the architect, a woman who also used to work at the megachurch firm. She talked for a long time about the house she was designing for a difficult client. "She's decided she wants to flip the whole floor plan around," the woman complained. Leah would be an easy client. The house she'd design would consist of four or five spacious, well-lit rooms, clear views from large windows, no obstructions. She would keep fresh flowers on the table and a piano in the corner. She would invite people over. She would do everything differently.

Therese perched next to her, on the arm of the couch. Alan brought out the martini shaker and refilled empty glasses. Leah, Alan and Therese were bunched up together, Alan pouring, the women holding out their glasses for him. Therese leaned into Leah and Leah leaned too, almost resting her head on Therese's shoulder. They could have all kissed each other. Leah and Therese clinked glasses, sloshing a little vodka on themselves. Alan offered a clean folded napkin from his pocket, and returned to the kitchen to make another batch of drinks.

"I'm so sorry about your husband," Therese murmured.

Her husband? At first Leah misunderstood—thought (absurdly) that Therese was talking about Alan, Alan as Leah's rightful husband. But, no. Therese meant Leah's dead husband. Alan must've passed along this juicy tidbit while Leah was upstairs. Married people, gossiping in the kitchen! Therese's comment was a rebuke, too, because Leah had never told her the story. Of course, Therese hadn't asked.

"I'm sorry I never mentioned him," Leah said.

Therese waved away her concerns, pecked her on the cheek. "We'll talk about it later. If you want. Or not." She went to tend to her dessert. Alan was back, refilling glasses. A thread dangled from the hem of his sweater. Leah imagined tying it to the coffee table leg, how he would walk around and around the room getting tangled up in the furniture, the legs of his guests. His sweater would unravel up to his armpits before he noticed. He smiled at her. The smile was almost a wink.

He would not tell Therese about their shared past. Leah understood. He would keep this secret, and would ask her to keep it too. Therese revealed everything, but Alan and Leah were alike: cards close to the vest.

Loud laughter filled the room. Leah had missed the joke, and smiled noncommittally. She set her drink on the table. From where she sat, she could see the entryway, the bench and the boots, the red sleeve of her coat. She would have to think up some excuse. She was tired, getting a migraine, expecting a phone call. She forgot something she was supposed to do, she had to get up early, she was terribly sorry.

Now the house took on the perilous and intricate quality of one of Leah's dream houses. The obstacles that lay before her were many. Trapezes and tightropes, secret rooms she would have to pretend not to notice, underground tunnels and passageways; a twisting and dark labyrinth home.

How About You Shut Up

How about 'Liam'?" The book of baby names lay open on her ever-widening lap. She hadn't decided whether she would marry the person sitting next to her—the father of the baby she hadn't planned, at first, on having. In some ways it would be a good idea—marriage.

He made a face. "Liam."

"Liam *Neeson*? Liam . . ." She couldn't think of any other examples.

"I'm just wondering about, you know, the locker room ramifications. The playground. The basketball court."

"What does that even mean?"

"Liam. It's kind of—foreign."

"Foreign?" she frowned. Flipped back to the I's. "How about Isaac, or Isaiah? I like those I-names."

"Irving? Irwin? Ignatius?" he read over her shoulder. He smelled charcoaly, like the hamburgers he'd made earlier that evening. She had a grill on her apartment terrace, but July in Oklahoma was hotter than anyplace she'd ever lived. Too hot to eat and way too hot to be eight months pregnant. She shifted her considerable weight, trying to get comfortable, which was impossible. Something was in his beard—a little white fuzzy thing. He often had things in his beard. He had a nice nose, though, and a decent job as a manager of a shoe store at the Sooner Fashion Mall. She would always have reasonable shoes. The baby could wear those miniature Nikes. And she liked his stories about his customers. He did funny imitations of the OU sorority girls whose daddies were rich oil men. Her own feet were swollen past recognition. She was wearing Birkenstocks, which they did not sell at his store. It wasn't that kind of store.

"Isaac is so Old Testament," he continued. "Look—'the son of Abraham and Sarah.'"

"It means 'he laughs' in Hebrew. That bodes well."

"We're WASPs, though." He touched his beard and dislodged the bit of fuzz without knowing it.

"You don't have to be Jewish to name your kid Isaac."

"What if the sonogram was wrong?" he asked. "Shouldn't we at least look at girls' names?"

She wanted a girl. But the technician had been certain. Had tapped the screen—while she lay in the dim room with cold goop all over her stomach—and said, "Thar she blows." Which, she thought, was the strangest thing possible to say about a fetus's unit.

She wanted a daughter because if she ended up being a single mother, it seemed easier to do with a girl.

"Jeff is a good name," he offered, when she ignored him.

"Jeffrey," she considered.

"No, I mean, just—Jeff."

"You *name* him Jeffrey, and then call him Jeff."

"Why? Why is that a rule?"

"You can't name someone a nickname. You give the person a real name, so he has the option, later, of using it. In case he wants to do something other than play basketball or run around at recess." How had she managed to get herself knocked up by someone who would put "Jeff" on his kid's birth certificate? How had she even managed to get through the appetizers, the salad?

She was being mean. She was churlish with the heat, the pregnancy, the decisions they had to make, decisions that sucked all the air out of the room. She imagined getting in the car and driving up north to her parents'. They had a house near Crane Lake, in Minnesota. It would be cool there.

He wanted to marry her. He wanted to be the dad. She appreciated that. She did.

"I still don't get why it has to be *Jeffrey*."

"It's not going to be Jeffrey, so drop it." They scanned the rest of the page. Jeremiah, Jericho, Jersey. He made a predictable jokey plea for "Jethro," and, predictably, sang the theme song to *Beverly Hillbillies*, complete with twangy banjo sound effects. He had a nice voice. Maybe their son would inherit his musical talents. Maybe he would play the cello. She had dated a cellist back in college. Now she was twenty-six. There weren't going to be any more cellists at this rate.

When he was done singing, she put small check marks, in pencil, next to Jonah, Joshua, and Julian. He started to protest, but she turned to the G's.

"How come we don't go in order?" he asked.

"What order?"

"Alphabetical. Why are we skipping around?"

She closed the book. "It's time for you to shut up now." She pushed herself off the couch like someone launching a boat from its dock. In the kitchen she spooned Braum's English Toffee ice cream into a bowl. She could feel him trying to decide whether or not he should follow her (and this made her feel sorry—how irritable she was toward him, how difficult). Finally he turned on the television; she heard the familiar sounds of a VH-1 countdown. She put away the ice cream—touched the snowy ice crusted on the freezer walls and pressed chilled fingertips to her face—and at that moment, her water broke. Right there in the kitchen. This doesn't always happen, she observed, as if to reassure herself. *Only about ten percent of pregnant women rupture the sac of amniotic fluid before labor begins.* Hers broke. Had broken. She ate a bite of the ice cream, looking at the floor and trying to remain in that odd calm place where she could pretend this wasn't really happening (a month early!) or was happening to some other pregnant woman in some other kitchen with some other boyfriend in the other room. Then she did the only thing, under the circumstances, she could think to do. She called out his name.

Thirty

I was twenty-eight when I knew, finally, that I would leave Gabe, and when I was thirty, I left him. The first Persian Gulf war had just begun, and a group of us sat in a Tonganoxie bar on a foggy night—we never have fog in Kansas, but that night it was foggy and atmospheric, as if the world had gone blurry outside the large plate glass windows—and we watched Dan Rather on a television above the bar give us the bad news. We had grown up during the Vietnam War. We remembered the body counts on our TV screens every night. It didn't seem possible that this new war could have been declared, as if it had happened when we weren't looking.

The war was not a metaphor for my personal life in ruins. The war was the war. My friends bought me drinks because I had left the man I had lived with for years—all of my adult life. My misspent youth, I liked to call it. But it wasn't entirely like that. The situation with Gabe was complicated, as situations generally are. (I loved him. But.)

In order to depart, I needed a catalyst. The catalyst was named Derick. He did not show up at the bar that January night, the first night of the war, as I had expected. His absence should have been a clue. I watched the grainy black and white footage on the television, the eerie explosive flashes streaking across the screen, Dan Rather's grave expression, and tried to ignore the people entering and exiting the bar.

I had moved from Gabe's farmhouse in the country into the town of Lawrence, into one of those generic apartment complexes, a kind of blank place for sorting yourself out. The buildings were named after French provinces: Bretagne, Normandy, Champagne, Anjou. I lived in the Dauphine. The place was lousy with divorcees. Next door to me lived a former Miss Indiana, a good twenty years older than I was, with a grander apartment than mine—fireplace, white sofa, plush carpeting. Occasionally we were both on our terraces at the same time, and lifted our drinks in greeting, then pretended the other person wasn't there, so as to offer each other the semblance of privacy. The man who visited her on weekends—I thought of him as her gentleman caller—had the slushy and lurching voice of a drinker, the kind of date I knew something about. My neighbor and I never introduced ourselves. Still, if we had been characters in a movie, and I was watching us, I'd get what the director was saying: if I wasn't careful, my life would turn out like my neighbor's one day, without the former beauty queen title.

Those were confusing days. What do I remember?

I remember reading Derick's book. He had given me a copy before I left Gabe, four hundred or so manuscript pages bound with a rubber band. A novel he had written—a book about Vietnam. He didn't have an agent or a publisher, but he was hopeful, he was taking creative writing classes, he was getting advice from professors.

I wanted Derick to be brilliant. I also wanted to have sex with him. You could say I was a friendly reader.

But I thought that was the point. I thought I had left Gabe so that Derick and I could finally be together. And then he didn't meet me at the bar and he didn't call me on the day I moved into the new apartment.

He had the phone number. He had the address.

Perhaps he was nervous. Perhaps he was waiting for me to call and say how smart he was, how good the book was. I don't know. I don't remember thinking about things from his point of view. How it would feel to have a woman he didn't know all that well leave her boyfriend, to be with him. How it would feel to know she was expecting something. A phone call, for instance.

Perhaps I miscalculated the extent of his interest.

I didn't care about the Vietnam stuff so much. I'd read some Vietnam novels and I wasn't sure you could do any better than the novels I had read. I was looking for other evidence, scouring the prose for signs, for pertinent information. Girlfriends, lovers, wives. I skipped ahead. I didn't find much that was useful.

Meanwhile, I had left *Gabe*. I was sick with grief and shame and also sick with longing. That feeling when you've done something and you can't quite believe you've done it.

As I read Derick's pages, hurrying along, waiting for the good parts, I kept looking up, surprised to find myself in that apartment with its white walls and freshly shampooed carpeting and new kitchen appliances and new smells. It was like jolting awake, over and over again. That Dauphine apartment was nothing like home.

Home was Gabe's farmhouse. His house. His house when I moved in, and his house when I moved out. His house still. He lives twenty miles outside of town. The house, a hundred years old, made of stone, is surrounded by fields and farmland and pasture. Even now I dream about it. In the dreams Gabe has always renovated extensively. The rooms he has added since I lived there go on and on. The rooms are proof that it is not my house anymore. I recognize almost nothing.

Gabe didn't want me to leave. My leaving surprised him. We had spent a long time drifting in our noncommittal way, month to month, year to year. Nothing changed, really, or the changes were so small we hardly noticed them. It was comfortable, yes. But I had to do something. I wasn't a young girl anymore. I was almost thirty.

And then, once I left he said okay, he'd marry me, yes, he'd have children with me, let's have them right now, let's start today. In the ensuing weeks, he called me on the phone or came to the Dauphine, and sometimes we even went out to eat together, we went to movies, we went for coffee, we went for drinks. Sometimes I thought I should go back to him. I longed for those stone walls and the blue-tiled counters in the kitchen and the delicate green pattern on the living room wallpaper, the wood floors and the tall windows looking out onto the weathered barn and cottonwood trees and pasture, the milo ripening a deep brown red in the fall and in the winter, the startling bright green patches of winter wheat against the gray and brown hills.

And Gabe. When I explain about Gabe, I sometimes use shorthand. I say, *alcoholic.* But his drinking wasn't why I left. And leaving wasn't about the possibility that he was having an affair with a lab technician at work—a woman whose bikinied image I would later see taped to my (Gabe's) refrigerator in my (Gabe's) house—because I didn't know about her when I left, or I knew about her but he swore they weren't involved, and I believed him, because I believed he would tell me the truth if I asked him straight out.

But it isn't about her. It isn't about the difficulties of living in that house—the well going dry during summer droughts, no heat in winter except the woodstove, a gravel road that washed out every spring and left a quarter mile of mud where the car got stuck up to its axles and me late to one dead-end job or another. It isn't even about Gabe not wanting to get married.

No.

I was thirty. I had finally begun to understand about one thing leading to another. About cause and effect. This choice leads to this choice leads to this.

Is that it?

Or: I had begun a friendship, a flirtation, with Derick, and once I started, I couldn't stop. Didn't want to stop. Didn't have to stop.

Or: I ran away from home. I ran away from home for the reasons people run away.

Or: I was too young to . . . I wanted . . . I loved Gabe, but . . . Stupid Derick.

He knew where I was living now. Why didn't he come see me? He had wanted me to leave Gabe. He had kissed me outside a bar where we went to talk, and he had kissed me another time outside his house, and that time he wanted me to go inside his house and I said I couldn't. I would leave Gabe first, I said. I had thought about leaving him for months, and now I would leave him. And this man kissed me and said, I want you to leave him. I want you.

Still, once I had managed the difficult task of leaving, he did not call.

That first night alone, reading the manuscript pages like a code I was trying to crack, I knew very well that this was my chance— that having finally left Gabe, I could do anything I wanted. I could move to a different place. I could go back to school. I could travel, find a job overseas, learn a new language. I could start over.

And instead? I sat in my apartment, waiting for the phone to ring.

So finally, I called Derick. He came over. We talked about his novel.

We had initially disappointing, then later, thrilling sex.

Derick's house was small, compact, a one-story house eight blocks from the Dauphine. I walked those blocks, back and forth, many times during the next year. Derick had insomnia, since his wife had left him. He was fidgety and restless and didn't want to disturb my sleep, he said. So we did not spend the night together, except once or twice, accidentally.

On Friday nights we met at a bar we especially liked. Derick's graduate student friends were there and sometimes my old friends from before. When I was with this group I felt as if I were the oldest one, not Derick. I was the one with the real job—I worked as a conference planner at the university—while everyone else was a graduate teaching assistant, living with roommates, going to classes, sitting around coffee shops. Fridays meant drinking with Derick, but not going home with him. Going out but not *together*. I drank too much trying to keep up with him, thinking he might leave with me when I left. He didn't.

On Saturday nights, I cooked dinner for him. We talked about his time spent in the army. We talked about his first marriage. We talked about his writing. We talked about his stepchildren who lived in California. We talked about our separate futures, occasionally allowing the plans to run parallel to each other, so that we would each, separately, talk about traveling to Japan to teach, or spending a summer in France, but we would never speak about those things as if we were going to do them together. Often we went to his house to watch a movie because I didn't have a television. We rented videos, and he did funny imitations of actors. He put wads of tissues in his cheeks and did a wicked Marlon Brando. "I coulda been *some*body." He liked to perform for me, and he made me laugh. Then we went to bed, then we listened to a blues show on the university public radio station, then I walked home, then I waited until the next Friday to see him again.

At work during the week, I tried to make plans for the evening ahead: I'd go jogging, make stir-fry for dinner, see a movie, sign up for a yoga class. On my way home I sometimes passed a small group of anti-war protesters, standing on a busy corner with their poster board signs raised or their lit candles in hand. I knew most of these people. I felt guilty for not standing with them, for not being part of their peace vigils and increasing their numbers by one, anyway. I was too involved in my personal drama, too consumed with this terrible hunger. I had no energy for anything else. I honked and waved at my friends in support, or if I felt especially ashamed, I drove a different route home. The hours between six and bedtime seemed almost impossible to get through. The apartment was too small. I could hear Miss Indiana's television; she was a journalism professor, and kept CNN on all the time. Wolf Blitzer's voice came through my walls at all hours. I bought earplugs. I missed my old house. I missed the country, where I had never been this unhappy. I tried to decide if that was a sign: I had been less unhappy there, so perhaps I should go back. I wasted time all evening, not doing any of the things I had planned to do.

One of the few times I slept at Derick's house, I woke up in the middle of the night alone. It was a hot night in July, and Derick's air conditioning wasn't working. I put on a T-shirt and went out to the kitchen.

And I took this picture in all at one time, it just met me there all at once, so that I understood something in one instant that I hadn't understood before, and blamed myself for not seeing it. Derick was leaning against the counter smoking a cigarette, a can of beer in his hand. Only the stove light was on. He turned when I came into the room. The way he turned, the smile he gave me, how the features of his face had blurred and the sound of his voice and the way he said *sweetheart*—he never used terms of endearment with me, but here he was, leaning against the counter saying, "Hey, sweetheart." And I saw what had happened. He had gotten up in the middle of the night to drink even though we had been drinking all evening and gone to bed together, drunk, and passed out together. He was glad to be drinking alone, ruminating in his small dark kitchen. The drinking never made him sick in the morning. He was smiling and happy and drinking and smoking, and not with me.

This again, I thought.

But of course, the *sweetheart*. The smile. I opened a beer.

Late that summer Derick read in the paper about a movie that was to begin shooting in Kansas City. The casting agent was looking for extras, so he asked me to take some pictures. He didn't have any 8 x 10s, like real actors. He didn't have a camera. I brought my camera to his house. I took some pictures of him standing and some sitting and some close-ups of his face. He took one of me sitting on his porch. I had a new haircut and sat on the porch where we drank beer, sat there with my brand new haircut and he took my picture. I would like to see that picture now. I would like to see what was in my face.

Derick sent his pictures to the agent. The agent called him. She loved his look, she said. The slender build, the ponytail, the large sad blue eyes. He would be in a scene in a veterans' hospital. He might even have a close-up. He was to report to a certain location on a certain day. He was very excited. I knew then that someday I would sit in a movie theater, alone, waiting for his face to fill the screen.

But Derick had phobias about driving. He didn't like being on the highway. Sometimes he took medication. The day of his shoot I thought about him, driving the forty miles to Kansas City. I worried about him having to pull over to the shoulder, get out of the car and walk around in the August heat. Or maybe that would make the anxiety worse. I wished I could go with him, do the driving, help. Instead I thought about him all day. I worked hard at sending him positive energy, to get him from the car to the highway to the shooting location. I spent my lunch hour focused on transmitting that energy. I only ate half my salad, I was so busy transmitting.

When I called that night to see how it went, he said, "Oh, I didn't go."

He had decided not to go.

I began to think I should go back to Gabe.

He was seeing the lab tech, the woman from work. But when we saw each other or when we talked on the phone, he said, "Come home. I'll break up with her. I want you to come home." So somehow I believed that even though he was seeing someone else, the door was still open, the blue-tiled counter still bore my handprint, the furniture and record albums and pictures and cooking utensils I had, in my haste, left behind, held my place for me. I had two homes, one I had left, one I was merely inhabiting, and I could live in either one. I just had to pick.

In September I took an afternoon off. I had to go to the doctor. I had some bad tests. When my appointment was over I drove to Gabe's house. I still thought of it as our house, though I had not been there in months. I knew he was at work, and that I could visit the house without him knowing. I maneuvered the potholes in the gravel roads easily—muscle memory, flick the steering wheel this way, back that way. I parked where I always parked, underneath the hackberry trees. Lucy, my dog, was there. I couldn't have a dog in the apartment. Lucy had been our dog, but mine mostly. She was a badly behaved dog, always guarding her food too zealously so that sometimes I was afraid of her. Still when she greeted me, I realized how much I missed her.

We always kept the door unlocked. There isn't any point in locking your door in the country—if people want to break in, which they never do, they could just heave a rock through a window. The door pushed open now in the same old way, with a little vacuum suck and the curtains over the window fluttering. I walked into the house as if it were my house. Much of it was as I remembered. First the coolness—the kitchen had been added to the outside of the house, so the walls were stone and the room always cool. Then the blue counter and the oak table we had picked up at an estate auction, and the hutch where I kept the pressure cooker for canning tomatoes and the large casserole dish I used for corn on the cob, and the hand-blown glasses we had bought in Mexico. But also, taped to the refrigerator, a picture of the lab tech in a yellow bikini. On the counter, a suggestive greeting card signed in her plump girlish writing. Upstairs in my wicker trash basket, an empty condom box. I walked through all the rooms, touching the walls, the couch, the wide and deep windowsills, the doorframes, the things I had loved and taken care of. I sat at my table in the quiet house for a long time.

Because of the bad test results, I had to go to the hospital for minor surgery. *Mild dysplasia. Cone biopsy.* The test is often the cure, they said. By removing the sample tissue, they often got rid of those pre-cancerous cells. I stayed home from work for the rest of the week. I was supposed to rest.

The week before I had said something to Derick. I tried to talk to him. He hated that kind of talk, wasn't ready, he always said. So now I had been in the hospital, and I had come home from the hospital and he knew I was home. And he didn't call. He would probably attribute his silence to his own shame, our conversation had shamed him, or else his anxiety problems, how the hospital was another place that made him phobic, and then I would be comforting him again, I would be telling him it was all right. Or he would say that he thought that I wanted him to back off. "Didn't you say I was your transition person?" he asked me once. I looked at him. He was mixing me up with someone else! I would never have said that. It wasn't how I felt at all. It was not what I wanted or even what I wanted to want, though of course it should have been.

Those were large and whole days that I lived right inside of. Three of them, round and simple, solid, perfect, like objects you could walk around in or just lie down in and the rooms hushed and clean, the people in the other apartments all gone to work during the day, and no phone calls and no mind-numbing job and no drinking and no lover and no war. I was safe and clear and I didn't have to speak or walk or get dressed or even eat or leave the apartment or get up from the couch or open my eyes or close them. I didn't have to want anything. I didn't have to speak or see or act in any way that would lead to regret. I didn't have to walk the eight blocks. I didn't have to move. I needed rest. They told me that, on the discharge sheet. Three days rest.

I had surgery. After surgery, he didn't call me.

How simple! How clear! Problem solved!

A month later, on a cool evening in October, Miss Indiana, holding a highball in one hand and a tin bucket of ashes from her fireplace in the other, stepped outside of her apartment and began her uncertain trek down the carpeted stairs. And stumbled. Lost her footing, somehow. I didn't see it happen. I heard it, from inside my apartment, where I was filling out graduate school applications at my table. Heard *her*. A strange surprised cry, and then the flailing, falling body.

I could tell—from how she was lying at the bottom of the stairs—that she had broken her neck. I had no doubt about this. After I called 911, after they took her away, covered in soot, her slinky turquoise robe not tied quite shut (I wished I had been brave enough to close it properly for her), I cleaned up the ashes, the ice cubes, the scotch. At the top of the stairs, both of our apartment doors were open. I was trembling, of course, terribly shaken. But I went quickly through her rooms. I took her Johnny Walker from the kitchen counter, her prescription bottles of Percoset, Valium, and Lithium from the medicine cabinet. CNN was still on, Wolf Blitzer shouting into the empty white room. I turned off the television and shut her door.

I threw away her stash. Then, in need of comfort, or perhaps just because I knew he wouldn't be able to resist this good a story, I called Derick.

The affair ran its course.

Shortly after my neighbor's death, I was relieved to find myself growing tired of Derick. One evening we were at my apartment. We were angry, and after sex we hardly spoke. I washed some dishes. He got dressed, finished his beer, smoked a cigarette at my table. I watched him from the kitchen. I had met someone else, though nothing had happened with the new man yet. His name was Sean. I met him at a party. I was having car trouble, and Sean offered to help me get my car to the shop the next morning. I couldn't imagine Derick ever helping me like that. With Derick, I would have been on my own in that situation. When I looked at him sitting there, smoking, in his usual muddle, I was overcome with irritation. I knew it was the last time we would be together, though nothing was said.

In the weeks that followed there would be phone calls, a couple of letters, but at that moment, nothing. When he left, I didn't watch him go down the stairs—the same stairs that had killed my neighbor—through the peephole, as I sometimes did. I didn't see him push the bar on the building door. I didn't see the rectangle of parking lot light absorb him. I didn't watch as the door, in its halting way, closed in stages behind him. I stepped onto my terrace. My neighbor's railings had recently been strung with red, white and blue Christmas lights. I hadn't met the new tenant—the name on the mailbox was a woman's, another divorcée, I'd heard— and knew, also, that I wouldn't bother.

The lab tech moved in with Gabe. She had two children from her first marriage, whom Gabe later adopted. Derick graduated, sold his house, and moved to Wyoming. Sean and I started dating, and eventually married. I had a baby. My life became the life of a happier person. I quit my job, went back to school, had a second child, and got a job I like, teaching English as a second language at the university.

I'm forty-one now. Another war is going on, or maybe it's an extension of the first war; I'm not clear about how this one happened, either, and no one can explain it to me to my satisfaction.

I never dream about Derick, but I still dream about Gabe. In each subsequent dream, the farmhouse grows larger. The house is now the size of a resort hotel. The rooms go on and on, one after the other. In the dream Gabe shows me all the work he's done, catalogs all of the improvements. I decide to move back in with him. I realize that this is my home after all. I forget that I'm married to someone else and have children. Gradually my real life begins to seep into the edges of the dream, and then I have to decide all over again whether to leave Gabe and my house, or whether to stay.

Chicken Man

Now her name was Felicia Leighton, and she had left that old life behind. She was married to a chiropractor, had two children, lived in a white house with pillars. Every morning she listened to Mozart for twenty minutes, followed by ten minutes of Patsy Cline, followed by five minutes of Nirvana. In the summer she wore DKNY sandals that she kicked off in the car, preferring always to drive barefoot, the balls of her pedicured feet massaging the pedals, the radio loud. She was beautiful, Texan, blonde, and her husband had a huge inheritance, and she liked to say this sentence to herself: *the Leightons own half this town*, because it was dramatic but true. Felicity Joy was her real name.

From here, her breakfast room on a Monday morning in June, Felicia could see her gardens, the little Japanese bridge and the koi pond and the flowerbeds, the fountain, the gazebo, she had to have a gazebo—ever since *The Sound of Music*, I am sixteen going on seventeen. She had gotten all her ideas from the best magazines, she had studied them and clipped pages and kept everything in a manila envelope, and then she had drawn her own design and hired landscapers from the best nursery in town to do the work.

Though maybe it was too much. She felt the old panic

coming on. The gazebo was overkill. The copper sculpture. The waterfalls. Maybe she had gone too far. The medical doctors' wives—how they would gloat over their Kendall-Jackson at the club! No, everything would be fine, she breathed in, she breathed out, the Garden Tour was on Saturday and she would have her moment of glory, she would wear the Vera Wang knock off—no, wrong, she would go with something simple, they could not say she was putting on airs. She would shop today for some understated jewelry, yes, she breathed, shopping would certainly help. And she had the whole morning, thank God—Vacation Bible School started at nine, the children would be squared away until noon. She put four frozen chocolate chip waffles into the toaster oven, checked the time, called up the stairs, "Michael Leighton! Let's go! Madison! Bring down your hairbrush, honey, and that checkered pink ribbon."

On Felicia's right buttock was a butterfly tattoo. Sometimes, she swore, it itched. She wanted to have it removed, but Beau, her husband, wouldn't let her. He made her do stripper routines, though she had never really been a stripper. He liked to pretend her job as a waitress in a topless bar in Wichita Falls was a stripper job, no matter how many times she reminded him that she was seventeen when she had that job and desperate and it was not anything that she was proud of and she only did it for five months. He liked making her sit in a chair naked with her knees drawn up to her chest while he looked at her with a penlight he kept on his keychain. He liked aligning her back.

Felicia yanked open the toaster oven door before the ding, dealt the waffles like cards onto plastic plates, squeezed syrup recklessly from the plastic bottle, set plates on the table. She poured orange juice into cups, Tropicana with No Pulp and Calcium. When she was growing up they drank generic Tang. Her mother bought huge jars of the awful powder. "It's what the astronauts drink," she had insisted just about every morning of Felicia's childhood. Felicia's children had never met her parents. Her father was long gone, her mother had died the year Felicia started working for Beau as a receptionist. She pictured her soft-skinned children playing in the scrubby burned out yard where she had grown up, that tiny patch of weeds and burrs and crabgrass that turned crunchy and brown by the fourth of July. She could hear their whining: There's nothing to do! It's so hot! Everything's so ugly!

The children bumped and shoved their way to the table, Michael holding his Gameboy with both hands as if it might fly off, Madison twirling and pulling her hair, a habit that had left her with a bald patch on the right side of her head. "Maddie, you're doing it," Felicia warned. Madison dropped her hand automatically, then started in on the other side. Felicia took the brush and arranged her daughter's hair, a big bow on top of the bare spot. "Don't touch, okay, honey? Just try not to touch."

"Pretty soon she won't have any hair left at all," Michael observed in a philosophical tone. "We'll have to change her name to Fuzzy Wuzzy."

"Hush and eat. We need to get going."

Felicia was putting away the orange juice when the doorbell rang. She sighed dramatically as if people were always ringing her doorbell, and when would she ever get a minute's peace. She did a quick check in the hall mirror, teeth for lipstick, nose for stray stuff, and disabled the alarm.

A man stood on the steps. He was wearing a yellow knit short-sleeved shirt and freshly ironed khakis and his face was tanned, creased, some hard living there maybe, but with the light blue squinty eyes of someone accustomed to peering down fairways. More remarkably: He was holding a live, brown-red chicken. The bird looked like the bird in The Little Red Hen. Felicia stared, uncomprehending.

"Good morning, Mrs. Leighton. I hope I'm not coming at a bad time?"

It must be drugged, she thought, for the chicken stayed

tucked under his arm as quiet as a cat. "What on earth—" for now she noticed the man had placed a skillet on the doorstep, the kind of cast iron skillet that cartoon wives hit their husbands over the head with.

"Just thought you might be hungry. Thought you might could use a little something for lunch." He held the chicken out to her. It began its predictable stupid clucking and flapping and pecking—not sedated after all.

Felicia recoiled. Was this some kind of joke? Had her husband pissed off another patient? She started to shut the door (the children behind her in the kitchen shouting, who is it mommy? who is it?), but the man—there was something about this man—stopped her. "Wait just a moment, please, Mrs. Leighton—"

She opened the door just enough to see him, not crazy looking per se, not bug-eyed or wall-eyed or grubby. "Are you nuts, or what?" She heard her speech fall down the dark hole of her old Texas drawl, as if the sight of the chicken had called up her old life, which it had, since feeding chickens and collecting chicken eggs from a chickenshit-filled chicken coop and selling those eggs in her front yard had been an integral part of her girlhood.

The man smiled. He spoke softly, as if sharing an important and slightly embarrassing secret. "I fed this chicken by hand. I raised it from a chick, only the best grains and organic corn and specially formulated chicken feed, so you could chop off its head—"

Felicia slammed the door. Coffee bile rose halfway up her throat. What the hell was that about? She looked around her formal sitting room—she liked calling it her parlor—as if reminding herself where she lived. Oil portraits of the children hung over the couch, but otherwise they were not allowed to set foot in this room. The idea was to keep it *impeccable*, for when normal people came to call. She smoothed her silk sarong, her palms damp, adjusted a bobby pin that held the twist in her hair. She looked through the peephole. The chicken man stood in the circular driveway, surveying the windows of the house, smiling and shaking his head, as if he had gotten what he came for. The bird was calm again in his arms. When Felicia looked out a moment later he was gone, but the skillet, a dull black with a small hole in the handle for hanging, sat on the front step, a single uncracked brown egg rolling around in it.

Of course now they were late to church.

"Who was that at the door?" Madison asked. Her bow was already lopsided, her fingers busy.

"Someone. He had the wrong house." Felicia, still flustered, wished she had time to sneak just one tiny cigarette (the pack of Marlboros hidden inside the snow blower in the garage), but they were late again. She tried not to yell at the children even though they kept forgetting things they needed to do like pee. By the time they reached the church, the parking lot was filled with the usual SUVs and mini-vans. This year's VBS theme was Racing with Jesus. The church had even arranged for a real stock car to sit in the parking lot all week, with every Vacation Bible camper getting a turn to sit in the driver's seat. Felicia paused as they walked by the sleek red car, ran her finger along the painted flames.

Inside the sanctuary she made a quick tally: Karen Boone, Marcie Huddle, Janie McGraw, Sally Yates, all wives of physicians in town, all on the Garden Tour committee. They had arrived early of course, their children lined up in the front pews, bumping shoulders, restless from waiting. Felicia waved at Marcie, who was scanning the crowd like a cheerleader at a basketball game. Marcie waved back, then said something to the other women, and the tight little circle turned as one body to look at Felicia. "Jesus Christ," Felicia muttered through her smile, waving. She found seats for the children, and waited through the Christian Education Director's prayer and announcements. The teachers (volunteers) were introduced individually and applauded, the children divided into their age groups and led off to their classrooms. The mothers waved and called out last-minute admonishments, then stepped into the June morning—sweet freedom, a whole morning free! Felicia put on her sunglasses, her arms already tingling, anticipating the mall.

At the jewelry counter everything became clear, each object its own exact shape, as if the world had just come into focus— the racks of earrings, the display cases with their necklaces and watches, the beads and gems and chains and pins precisely themselves. Felicia bathed in the department store glimmer, inhaled the gently perfumed air, saw herself illuminated by the shiny warm light and felt calm and whole and good. She tried on necklaces, smiled at the saleswoman, complimented her haircut, and her fingers did not tremble as they slipped a thick gold bracelet into her waiting purse. She paid cash for a gold choker, pretended to write down the name of the clerk's hairstylist, and watched a coiled, silver-braided chain spill from her palm like water, just spill into her purse noiselessly, perfectly. Now the men's department for ties, and the heavy scent of cologne on the salesman there; she moved solemnly, stroking the things she wanted before taking them, then taking them, until she felt the liquid thing she had come here to feel. She wanted to rub up against somebody! She wanted to make out in someone's convertible, parked in a city she had never been to, her Chanel dress unzipped in the back, no bra! She had almost forgotten the morning's incident, the red hen, the skillet she had picked up with a Williams-Sonoma waffle weave dishtowel and thrown into the trash (the dishtowel too).

But as she turned toward Better Dresses she saw him, the chicken man, standing by the evening gowns, and felt herself slapped awake.

He smiled, his teeth very white, bleached maybe or else dentures, though he wasn't old. He had seen her, she was sure. No one else had been watching, but he had. She was about to bolt, but reminded herself that she was Felicia

Leighton now and nothing anybody said, certainly not this grifter or drifter or whatever he was, could make a bit of difference.

She walked right up to the chicken man. "Are you following me?"

"Mrs. Leighton," he said, still sarcastic about her name she noticed, "don't you believe in wild coincidences? I just happened to be out shopping this morning, looking for some jewelry, and a couple of . . . ties." He smiled again, that too-bright smile, and in the smile and in the voice she caught something familiar.

"Do I know you? Did you used to live down in Wichita Falls?"

"Wichita Falls? No, nope, never lived there. Why would you say Wichita Falls?"

"You are harassing me. I can call the police."

He looked pointedly at her bag. "Not such a good idea, is it?"

"Are you security or something? A detective?" Felicia glanced back at the clerk in the men's department but he was talking to another customer.

"Mrs. Leighton. Your secrets are safe with me."

Felicia felt a strand of hair slip from out of her twist and hooked it impatiently behind her ear. "Look. I don't know who the hell you are"—though this wasn't entirely true, for something in her mind was beginning to shift, like the turning over of mulch or laundry or a stubborn car engine, something was happening in there—"but you better quit following me around. I don't think you have any idea who you're messing with."

"Not so, Mrs. Leighton. I know exactly who I'm messing with." Beard, she thought. He used to have a beard. He reached up to tuck the escaped strand of hair back behind her ear. She jerked away, and he laughed, walked away laughing, shaking his head as if it were hard to believe just how much fun he was having. And the laugh—the laugh clinched it. She stood next to a magenta mother-of-the-bride gown, the treasures in her purse reduced to mere cereal box trinkets, the buzz completely wrecked.

Dwayne, she thought. Goddamn Dwayne Taylor.

Back then he had a beard. And long hair, and weighed at least thirty more pounds, and of course he was younger. She had only seen him that one night, and that had been over twenty years ago. But the laugh, yes—the derisive laughter. She remembered that.

She was fifteen. In love with Mitch Sullivan. Black Irish, Mitch used to call himself, dark curly hair and beard and green eyes and a face that said, I already know life is going to be hard, so bring it on. Mitch was eighteen. He had dropped out of school and worked, that year, at his stepfather's muffler shop. He smelled of car and oil and sweat. He worked Saturdays and so did Felicia, selling eggs in her front yard, while her mother held garage sales, selling off junk she picked up at flea markets and estate auctions. *Fresh Eggs*, a plywood sign read in black spray paint. Felicia sat in a lawn chair, furiously smoking her mother's Kools. She wore a halter top and hot pants, blue mascara and pale pink lipstick, platform red sandals. Boys from school drove by in rusted out Pintos and Gremlins and made rooster noises at her. She gave them the finger. Customers haggled over price, over freshness, but she stood firm and let them know from her cocked eyebrow and smirky mouth what she thought of them, even the old people. She collected their money in an old tin box. The box, she remembered, had a faded farm scene on it—black and white cows grazing under trees, sunlight shining through the leaves, a bucolic place that never existed. She hated that box and those stupid cows, that sunlit foliage. The smell of henhouse lay over the yard like a fog.

Saturday nights were her nights with Mitch, riding around town with friends, drinking beer in empty parking lots. Then Mitch got his own car, a second-hand pickup truck, and they set off on their own, driving to the subdivisions on the outskirts of town, where the rich people were building their new houses, huge houses on huge lots with no trees and no chickens. Mitch could sense which houses were empty—even the ones with the lights on were often unoccupied on a Saturday night, in summer, people at softball games or the movies or the lake. He carried with him a set of tools that released almost every lock they tried, but more often than not the rich people of that town were trusting, and a door—or at the very least, a window—was left unlocked. At first they just went in on a dare. They went out of curiosity. They went for somewhere to go. They played house: Mitch would take a beer from the fridge and yell, "Honey, I'm home!" Felicia made snacks (crackers and cheese, or a bowl of chips) and turned on the T.V. They didn't stay long in any one house, and Felicia was always careful to clean up afterwards.

Touring, they called it. *Let's go touring.*

As the weeks went on, they began to take things. Just little things at first: a ceramic pinch pot someone's kid had made in art class, a golf trophy, a framed picture of a baby from a guest room dresser. Felicia tried to find the single thing in every house that held the essence of someone who lived there. She kept her treasures in a box under her bed.

Mitch soon became interested in other items. Things he could sell to a guy he knew from way out in Midland. Stereo systems, televisions, coin collections, guns. They pulled two hauls like that without getting caught. Felicia didn't like it. She wanted to go back to just sitting on the rich people's leather couches, drinking a beer, eating Pepperidge Farm cookies, making out.

Then one night Mitch wanted to bring a friend from work, someone to help with the heavy lifting. A boy named Dwayne.

"You the girl with the eggs?" he asked Felicia, when they picked him up at his house. She thought he was being fresh, making some sex crack, and when she ignored him he laughed. He was like that, she remembered—laughing too loudly at the wrong times, so that nothing seemed fun that night.

At the last house, Dwayne followed her into the master bedroom, where she liked to see what people hid in their underwear drawers. He came up behind her and she assumed it was Mitch, standing there, so she leaned into him, lifting the strange small plastic object she had just discovered, then jerking around when she realized her mistake. "Don't run off," Dwayne said, grabbing her arm. "You know, Felicity Joy, the three of us could have a lot of fun together. Better than stealing." A picture came into her mind but she feigned disgust, pulled away.

In the living room, as they were getting ready to leave, Dwayne found a glass egg paperweight with a butterfly suspended inside. "Hey, Big Time," he said to Felicia, "this has your name on it." He tossed the egg to her. It was at that moment—as the egg sailed across the room and her hands reached up to catch it— that three police officers arrived, almost casually, as if it were a party and they'd been invited. "Fun's over, you little shits," a cop with a moustache said. They were frisked, handcuffed, all of it feeling to Felicia like something she had watched on television. Two patrol cars, lights flashing, waited in the driveway outside. Dwayne rode in one car, she and Mitch in the other. Before they reached the station, Mitch whispered three emphatic, careful sentences to her. "Dwayne got me into it. This was your first time. You came along for the ride."

She remembered it perfectly. The glass egg falling on the thick white carpet, bouncing twice; the policemen strolling into the room; the instructions Mitch gave her in the backseat of the patrol car, to save her.

And now Dwayne Taylor had found her.

The rest of the week was quiet. Felicia watched for signs of Dwayne, at the grocery store, at the Walgreen's, but he didn't show. She almost wanted him to. She kept to her routine, listened to her music, stayed away from the mall. It had been enough, perhaps, to bring her that chicken, and follow her in the department store, and now he had gone back to wherever he came from. She wondered where he did come from. She wondered if he knew where Mitch was, if Dwayne had played these games with him as well. She remembered without wanting to what it was like to have Mitch's hand reach slowly, slowly into her shorts, how wild she had been for him, how that part of her seemed dead now. In the mornings that week she watched Beau, her respected and respectable husband, walking around their property with that critical, almost predatory look. He was a good man, she told herself. He was a good provider, he was generous with money, he never raised a hand to her or the children.

But Beau Leighton was not an easy man to please. He wanted Angus beef or fresh snapper for dinner every night, the mail piled up just so in the basket, the sheets changed daily. He had gone through a half-dozen contractors in building their house. Walls had been torn down, built up, torn down again. Local people refused to work for him. Crews had to be hired from as far away as St. Louis. Felicia's job was to tell Beau he was right, he had been right to fire the good-for-nothings, and then she had to flirt with the new workmen to keep them from quitting. The whole thing had exhausted her. She thought of Mitch, how he would pounce on her and growl in this funny way, and how much she had loved that, their wrestling, the way he had tickled and teased her. He'd look in the mirror and whisper to himself, *You handsome motherfucker—don't you ever die.* Mitch had spent six months in prison; Dwayne was sentenced to two years; Felicia had done some community service, some probation time. She wrote to Mitch a few times but then started dating someone else, and then she got herself out of that town, and after another period of time she enrolled in a secretarial course and landed a job as receptionist for the man who later became her husband, which had taken some doing since he was already married to a pretty blonde when they first met.

On the morning of the Garden Tour, Felicia awoke early. She gave Beau a quick hand job so he'd be in a good mood. He took the children to the Perkins for breakfast, then to the park, agreeing to keep them away for the duration of the tour. Felicia showered and dressed, put on the white linen sleeveless dress she'd ironed meticulously the night before, the sling-back sandals, the new choker-necklace and gold bracelet. She took extra care with her hair and make-up, applying several coats of mascara. "You inherited my shitty eyelashes," her mother used to say, and it was true—eyelashes too light and thin to do much good. The mascara alone took her almost half an hour.

The Garden Tour committee supplied volunteer docents to offer information on each property, so Felicia didn't need to stay. But she wanted to. She greeted people and shook their hands and answered questions about the copper sculpture and the pond and the multiple types of day lilies until the docent, an older woman wearing a red, white and blue visor and a Tencel jumper, gave up and sat on the patio where she fanned herself with a Garden Tour program. Felicia began to think she had missed her calling. She should volunteer at an art museum and give tours; she was a natural; she could see before her a whole new kind of life. Through the breezeway that connected the front and back yards Felicia monitored arrivals and departures, and when a black pickup with no muffler pulled into the driveway, she knew who had come.

He was wearing overalls this time, a Feed and Grain cap, work boots—a costume. She reached him as he was stepping out of the cab.

"What are you doing here? I know who you are. I will go inside this very minute and call—"

Then she saw the crates. Five or six wooden crates in the back of the truck, filled with hens. Dwayne, a toothpick stagily sticking out of his mouth, began to unload the crates, and as he set each one on the ground, he opened it up and released the birds onto the perfect lawn. "Silkie Bantams. Very special breed. They make excellent pets." The hens were white, with a crest like a ridiculous hat on their heads; their feathers looked like Persian cat fur.

"What are you doing? What the hell are you doing?" Felicia heard her voice edging into the hysterical range. "My husband—do you know what my husband—"

Dwayne shook his head. He laughed. He unloaded the last crate. Now there were twenty, thirty Silkies pecking around the yard as if they had lunch reservations. The Garden Tour people, hearing the commotion, had begun gathering in the front yard, and exclamations filled the air, even screeches from some of the old women, as if the docile birds were rats or snakes.

Dwayne removed the toothpick from his mouth with a flourish. He leaned against the truck, crossed his arms, smiled. He spoke loudly, so the crowd could hear. "Here's your delivery, ma'am. Right on time. You have a real nice day."

Oh Lord, what would she do? All these people! Dwayne got back in the cab. She put her hand on the rolled down window. "Wait, Dwayne. Please."

He looked at her, she felt him taking her in, her eyes and mouth and the gold at her throat and ears and wrist, and her hair swept up, one lock slipping out of place. He smelled of aftershave and cigarettes. A picture of herself came to her, unbidden: Felicia in her white linen summer dress, walking around to the other side of the truck and opening the passenger side door and getting into the cab and slamming the door shut and driving down Main Street and past the church and the stores and the mall, out to the highway, the windows down, her hair flying, shoes tossed out the window, cigarette between her lips, her hand reaching for the bourbon that she knew would be underneath the seat. Beau would come home with the children and find the chickens in his yard and the empty crates in his driveway and the frantic docent flapping around the lawn.

Dwayne reached up and tucked the loose strand behind her ear, and this time she didn't pull away, even though people were watching, even though now there would be talk. She prepared her face and her story for the witnesses gathered, for she could do nothing else. An old joke from an old friend, she would say. Isn't it a riot? She turned to go, then had an impulse—leaned back into Dwayne's open window—flicked the clasp on the gold bracelet with one manicured fingernail—let it fall into his empty lap.

Wives

My first wife was a critical person. Pick, pick, pick. At first it was fun. Find the flaw and expose it to the light, like ticks off a dog that you burn in the ashtray, another fun thing we used to do. We lived in the country, and ticks were a problem. I was raising hunting dogs. I don't hunt much but I like dogs. A dog with a job—a hunting dog on a Saturday morning during quail season—that's a satisfied creature of God. It turned out the country wasn't the best place for wife number one. The house required constant repairs, and I was less interested in performing these tasks than she was in having them performed. While I was busy with the dogs and also my job in town (I worked in a frame shop), she had lost her position as a bank teller because she'd been offering free spiritual advice to the customers. Many people hadn't liked her take on things, and, as I tried to explain to her, you can't read people's auras without permission, and then expect them to be happy about it.

She was unemployed for two years. She had a lot of time to complain. She complained about my friends who liked to drop by on the weekends. Often, they didn't leave until Sunday night. Mondays were bad. She was especially hard on my friends' girlfriends and wives. Did you see the way she stuck her finger in her mouth to dislodge the food from her teeth? What did you think of her hennaed hair? She certainly is vulgar when she drinks. Eventually she became tired of picking on other people, and turned her considerable skills of analysis on me. Whoa! I never said I was perfect.

My second wife, therefore, was more easygoing. For every action there's a reaction. By this time I had moved into town. Wife number one received the country house in the divorce, and stayed in it just to spite me. I had to give up the dog business. I lived in one of those apartments on small town Main Street that's over a drugstore. It's the kind of place that, if you're just passing through, you wonder, Who would live there? Who passes by that drugstore every day, dusty boxes of ace bandages and tampons stacked forlornly on shelves, to open that glass door and climb up those dingy stairs? I'd like to think you'd be surprised to find out that it's a guy like me.

My second wife was gentle and accepting and worried about clogging the toilet. She had grown up with hippie parents, in a cabin whose septic tank was so sensitive they didn't flush the toilet paper. So she put the toilet paper in the trash can instead. She had long thick hair that she rarely washed, and thin ropy arms. At one time she'd been a violinist, but her right hand was broken in an accident at the restaurant where she worked, and she had to give up the violin. The sentence she uttered the most frequently was: "It is what it is." After wife number one, this was a pleasant philosophy to live with. But after a year, "it is what it is" put me into a murderous rage. Maybe it *isn't* what it is, I said. Maybe what it is *stinks* because you should be flushing it down the goddamn toilet.

My third wife was hardest on herself, and, come to find out, seriously OCD. Behavior therapy did not help. Drugs, only a little—she was catatonic then, instead of obsessive. Her hands were raw from washing. She had almost no fingernails. The bathing ritual after sex was elaborate and precise, and I had to help her. As soon as we started to make out, I'd begin projecting forward to the loofah, the cleanser, the latex gloves. It took ten times as long as the act itself, and after a while it was easier not to.

Wife #4: sane, not mean, tidy but not freakishly, employed, a good sense of humor. Her foul mouth didn't bother me as much as the angel wings tattooed on her shoulder blades, but you learn not to look. She fell in love with someone else and left me after six months.

Number 5? Who's going to marry a guy with four ex-wives, except someone with similar baggage? She had me beat, with five ex-husbands already—well, four exes and one dead, the only one she ever loved, but that feels too convenient even to me. She had a kid from each one: bam, bam, bam, bam, bam. I had no children from any of the wives, or from anyone else that I know of, and number five's were all out of the house by the time I came along, all except her last one, a seventeen-year-old kid who while under my roof brought older gentlemen into his room and charged them money to watch him beat off. "I was beating off anyway," he shrugged when I confronted him about his "friends." Wife #5 swore she knew nothing about it. She was a fun-loving sort but trying a little too hard now that she was past fifty. She loved the Indian Casino. Luckily, we kept separate accounts.

I live in the country now. Different house from the one where, I've learned, wife #1 still lives, though she came into some family money and had the whole place gutted and renovated, new everything. She never did remarry. She and I live in different states, but we've started to exchange emails. She has a lot to say about those early years, and how far she's evolved, and where her journey is taking her. Maybe we'll meet for coffee, somewhere along I-70, and amuse ourselves with the past while eating truck stop pie.

I'm raising hunting dogs again, Boykins this time. Wife #5's kids come to see me, though I've never asked them to.

They all look like their fathers, each face stamped with the respective nose/mouth/eyes combo. They come *en masse*, like Christmas carolers. I can barely keep their names straight. When I offer them a drink or the pick of the latest litter at a reduced price, they smile and shake their heads as if I've had trouble aplenty and should hang on to everything that's left, including the last inch of liquor in the bottle and the runts I can't sell. No argument there. When they leave, I wave from my porch, their cars like a funeral procession down the long driveway. The dogs in their kennels bark like crazy, and it sounds like laughter to me, it sounds like they are in on some joke.

What Happens Next

THE MAN IN THE GARAGE

A woman goes into her garage. She keeps an extra refrigerator there, for storing watermelons and party hors d'oeuvres. She is looking for a bag of frozen chicken that she knows she bought but cannot, now, an hour away from dinner, find. When she closes the refrigerator door (no chicken) she sees a man standing there, beside her husband's workbench. She is not frightened, and she understands, in the way you understand things in a dream, that the man is living there, in her garage. He is thirty-one (he says when she asks) but looks much younger. He has been using a sleeping bag that the woman recognizes as her son's. They store camping gear in the garage and the man has also uncovered a camp stove and a canteen. She does not tell anyone about the man but instead begins to bring him food, the way you would feed a stray cat living under your deck. When other people appear the man hides. Sometimes the woman thinks she is maybe imagining him. But each night when she comes out to the garage, smuggling food on paper plates, the man is there waiting for her, and smiles and thanks her and tells her it won't be long before he's back on his feet.

THE ANALOGY KING

He says, "It would be like leaving on a trip and forgetting your suitcase. It would be like if you loved mashed potatoes and all your wife ever served you was baked. It would be like finding the perfect woman and then finding out she was married to some jerk-off you used to work for. It would be like driving a new car off the lot and having all four tires fall off at the first intersection. It would be like seeing your old man for the first time in twenty years and having him ask you, first thing, so how much money you making now? That's what it would be like."

MANGO

She sits with the baby in the kitchen, early morning. The baby bangs his drooly hands on the tray of the high chair. He vocalizes. He jabbers. He squeals. She is alone, she is here alone with the baby not just today but from the beginning and always. Last night, around one in the morning, a wild storm ripped a branch from the elm tree in the front yard, and the branch crashed on her roof. She lay awake and felt, really, that she didn't think she could do it. She honestly wasn't sure she could do it. Not just the limb on the roof but the water bill, the balancing of checkbooks and work schedules, the grocery shopping, the worrying over fevers, over pink eye, over ear infections, over college entrance exams. But now, morning. She peels a mango. She is tired but not as tired as she thought she might be. The sun shines into brown puddles and bright leaves. The mango is slippery in her hands like a cool organ. The juice drips down fingers, wrists, forearms. She cuts the fruit. She sucks the large flat white pit, stringy mango between her teeth. She gives the baby a piece. He gums it, eyes wide at this new thing, hands already reaching for more.

FISH HOUSE

A couple goes to look at a house in the country. The realtor assures them it is perfect, it is just what they've been waiting for, their search is over, and will they please ignore the fish. When they get there they see what she means. Everywhere in and outside of the house there are fish. Goldfish, guppies, minnows. Plastic trash cans fill the yard, a dozen of them, water to the top, and if the couple looks closely they can see fish swimming deeply in the brackish water. The basement is crammed with tanks, tanks on every available surface, lined up on the floor, on tables, on shelves built specially for the tanks, the gurgling of the filters like waterfalls, like rapids, like static. Objects have been dropped into the tanks for effect: a hand-held mirror, a flowerpot, a billiard ball, a glass monkey. The woman feels tired at the prospect of the owner having to dismantle all the tanks. Once, the couple and their children went on vacation and when they came back, the fish in the tank in their daughter's room were all belly up. They had forgotten to tell the housesitter about the fish. What kind of people do this, they wondered about themselves, what kind of people forget their own daughter's pets when they go on vacation? Their daughter became a psychologist, which frightened them. They wanted, once their children were gone, to buy a house in the country, but they do not buy this one.

CORPORATE GUY

The girls. The business trips. The sports bars after eight-hour meetings in windowless conference rooms, conference calls, catered lunches, PowerPoint presentations. He keeps it separate, in its own box. Here is one. Here is the other. He keeps it going. He keeps it secret. He keeps it to himself. No one has to get hurt. Wife, daughters, house. Ex-wife, son, child support. Girls, work, hotels. Three boxes.

Easy? You think it's easy? You think he's proud of what he's doing? No. He's not proud. He doesn't understand it himself. He knows better. But he can't help it. That's really how it feels: He can't help it, maybe he's sick, maybe there's something wrong with him. He knows how he sounds, how the women in the room if they heard him would all roll their eyes, laugh in that mocking way women have now that they didn't used to have, yeah right whatever. But it's late. The girl. She's a consultant. Lives in another city, not his city and not even the city where they find themselves after a long day talking. Not talking the way you just talk. That kind of talking that he likes where everything means something else. A game, you drop a little something, she picks it up, she drops a little something, you pick it up, it's back and forth like that, it's just a game, and he's so good at it. He's so good! A born leader, a people person, a sure thing. Everyone says so. Hundred-dollar ties. Hand-sewn shoes. He's rising to the top. The money. The office. The car. The drinks. The hotel room, always hers so he can leave and sometimes (he tells his wife during the confession scene) sometimes he can't even get it up! Poor guy! He can't even get it up. Imagine how that feels, you think he's having fun doing this, you think this is fun, it's humiliating! And sometimes, could it be a blackout? That curtain drawn, that darkness between one thing and the other, and then in the morning . . . not being sure? When the girl looks at him over the thermal carafe of coffee? Not knowing? Having to pretend? You think that's easy?

And then, really, he's almost relieved, the airplane taking off, the flight attendant coming down the aisle with his drink, the hour or two hours or three with everything just suspended, just hanging there in the sky.

SAMPLER

Two mothers sit on the park bench. One is fat and one is thin. Their children, little boys who are both two years old, do not look like either of the women but take after their fathers. The fat mother's child wants to sit on her lap. The thin mother's child explores the swing, the sandbox, the baby slide. The women secretly hate each other. The fat woman hates the thin woman because she complains too much. The thin woman hates the fat woman because of her phony laugh. A teenager sits on a bench nearby, a girl with pierced lips and nose and eyebrow, small hoops hanging off of everything. She is doing cross-stitch, a sampler that says, in old-fashioned lettering, "One day at a time." The fat mother's boy wants to nurse though she weaned the boy three months ago. He does not consider himself weaned, however. When it is time to leave, the two women strap their babies into their car seats, gather up in their minds all the scraps of things the other woman said while they were talking, and take the scraps home for lunch.

A STORY A DAY

The writer, living alone now, writes stories. She has maybe lost something, a husband or a house or a job or a best friend or a beloved pet. The stories are on the edge of making sense but don't quite make sense. Everything the writer used to write made sense and now she tries this other thing. She writes one story a day. She cannot take one story from one day into the next but must start a whole new one, even though she knows this is not how it's done. Even she did not used to do it this way but worked steadily on one story for days or weeks or even months and years before the story was done. She wishes she could write poems because she believes it would be easier to write a poem a day but she can't write poems. She can only do what she does. She can only not look out the window too often or vary too much what she eats or where she goes. For diversion she has her morning and afternoon walks with the dog, whom she often says she loves more than any person she has ever known.

JELLYFISH DAY

The jellyfish arrive in the mail. On a postcard: floating, ethereal, poisonous, reminding me, as they were intended to do, of that day in the aquarium at the Omaha Zoo when the four of us stood around the jellyfish tank, watching the tentacles' slow-motion sweep. I could see the distorted faces of my children through the glass, and the face of my wife, with whom I hadn't had sex for over a year. (We were polite about it, kind to each other at bedtime, averting our eyes.) The strange creatures quieted us. They seemed to inhale and exhale with their whole bodies, puffy filmy boneless things, although I do not know that they breathe in this way, nor do I remember anything I might have read about their physiology on the information cards that day. What I remember is a momentary calm. How I did not reach to my back left pocket and tap my wallet with two of my fingertips a precise number of times, how I did not count tentacles or steps or breaths or seconds, how I did not think about choking or falling. I just stopped, stopped moving and my wife and my son and my daughter stopped with me.

The postcard is from my daughter, now sixteen. "We went on a field trip to the aquarium," she writes. Other things too. I put the postcard with the other ones. Go wash my hands.

REUNION

For the next six months she will eat only 1200 calories a day, and the best thing, she believes, is to break up those calories into four mini meals so that she does not feel deprived, and the way to succeed, she believes, is to keep a food diary and to write down every bit of food she consumes including the grilled cheese sandwich crusts and half-cookies left on her children's plates, she can see the dainty lists in the notebook she will buy just for this purpose, *half a grapefruit, half a bagel, 1/2 c. cottage cheese, four orange sections, green salad with 1/4 tsp. vinaigrette dressing,*

4 oz. broiled fish, and she will start exercising, walking at first, just a mile, she can push the baby stroller while the other kids are at school, and then gradually increasing to two miles and to jogging (she can buy a baby jogger) and to strength training and cross training (she can hire a babysitter) and she can see herself, magically shrinking, she can see herself, now, as she heats the baby's bottle and half-listens to the kitchen TV and watches out her window the landscape man planting shrubs around the house next door, and the dream of her new self is so clear before her, the way she will look, the way she used to look, although she never really looked that way, but she used to dream of looking that way, and it is the same look she dreams of now only her hair is lighter, and the drapey black dress in the catalog, and the new haircut, and the manicure; how it will be when everyone sees her, it will be worth every minute and every effort, and she sees herself already transformed, she sees herself the way she will look in six months after she has already faithfully done the exercising and faithfully stuck to the diet and she is already done, and as she crosses the kitchen, as she turns off the TV, as she wipes her hands, as she cuts herself a piece of Sara Lee, she feels almost happy.

TAKING A GEOGRAPHIC

This is what they say at AA meetings when someone moves away, tries a new life in a new place instead of staying in the old place with all the old problems.

WALKING WOMAN

Every day I see that woman with her dog. I don't know where she lives but she is everywhere I go. I'm in the car, driving to the store, she's walking the dog. I'm dropping my kids off at school, she's walking the dog. I'm driving to the post office, she's walking the dog. Does she have a twin, with a twin dog? She wears athletic bras and gray gym shorts and a visor and sunglasses. The dog, a husky mix, wears a harness. The woman apparently does not have any other life except this walking life, with its angry strides.

THE POINT JUST BEFORE THE POINT

Her skin smells like chlorine. She swims laps over her lunch hour and then meets him, here. When he kisses her neck, he dives into water. Her hair is still damp at the ends. She doesn't use blow dryers or wear make-up that will run in the water. They have gotten to the point in the affair just before the point where they stop talking about what they will do and know they will soon stop talking altogether. Their sex is almost sad but not sad yet or not any sadder than usual. Their faces, when they see each other, almost still register delight but not quite delight. He breathes in her bleached smell, he dives in again, he resurfaces, he does the backstroke, the sidestroke, the crawl.

SIGNS

Your baby is dehydrated or might be dehydrated or you should start thinking about the possibility of dehydration when the following symptoms occur, and these are listed from mild to severe, with mild meaning that your appropriate reaction will be similarly mild and you can certainly wait until morning to call your pediatrician's office and speak to a nurse who will advise you first before making an appointment, to severe in which case you need to be in the emergency room within thirty minutes (and bring the record you've been keeping, with the baby's weight recorded each day and the input and output of the baby's input and output recorded there in the correct columns): tacky or sticky roof of mouth, crying without tears, less frequent urination, dry pale wrinkled skin, red lips, sunken eyes, mottled skin, cool hands and feet, rapid pulse, dark urine, lethargy, disorientation, tacky or sticky roof of mouth. Get help immediately.

PLAN A

He emails his wife that they are getting a divorce. He writes it like a memo. To: From: Re: He cc's his lawyer who was also the best man at their wedding and also his roommate at college. She accepts the financial arrangement. She can't think what else to do. She considers exhaust fumes in the garage or enough sleeping pills to knock down an elephant, but the children. She remembers an old friend saying, "Why kill yourself? Wait around and see what happens. Go to Mexico. Take up skydiving. Get a dog." So she tries Mexico first. She goes to Mazatlán. She eats at Señor Frog's with all the license plates from different states on the walls, though she is too old for this sort of place. She loses a sandal on the beach. She drinks Coronas with lime wedges stuck into the necks of the bottles. The ocean is close enough to the hotel pool that you can smell and hear it. The ocean is loud and clear. She misses her children and flies home after two days. He has taken all his clothes and his baseball trophies and his collection of first editions from the house. She has the locks changed, she has her hair cut, she has her eyes done, she has the decorator in, she sells the house, she moves to a new house, she enrolls in a horticulture therapy class, she contests the custody arrangement, she goes to a support group, she buys one of those cute VW Beetles (lime green), she takes up tennis, she colors her hair, she colors it back again, she gets a bikini wax, she goes to a chiropractor, she goes to a personal trainer, she goes to a singles group, she goes on three bad dates, she takes the children to a therapist, she returns to court, she refuses to become bitter, she refuses to let the fact that he is already remarried to a woman with two children the same ages as the children they had together bother her, she refuses to let the fact that his new wife is pregnant with another child bother her, she refuses to let the fact that she is about to turn forty bother her, she refuses to let the fact that she is (as she looks around at her friends) a dime a dozen bother her. If, she tells herself, she still feels this way next year, she will try the skydiving, and then the dog, and after that it's back to Plan A.

WHAT HAPPENS NEXT

Advice comes in from everywhere, flying in through the open windows and slipping under doors. Friends call, friends email, friends stop by. They make her coffee. They bring her food in disposable containers and store it in her freezer with the other disposable containers full of food. They pick up her kids, her dry cleaning, her car from the shop. They do what they can. After a while they get bored. She understands, she knows that everyone else is still existing in a moving-forward time and can't be expected just to drop everything. Of course they feel bad for her, they feel guilty. But, the friends all say, the children are old enough to help. The children are in high school now. The children, twins, a boy and a girl, go in their rooms and shut their doors. The children eat at friends' houses. The children drive themselves to and from school. The children apply to college. They decide to go far away. They decide to move to the west coast. She hears them in their rooms, packing. She hears them leaving. Goodbye, goodbye! The dog, not the one from before because he died but a new one with a similar name, sighs.

Camille's Country

My sister sends me letters from Africa. They arrive every week, ripped open by the censors, taped clumsily shut. It is a dangerous thing, to write, but Camille has always been reckless. The government in her country is weak, perhaps about to fall. Camille can't talk about it directly. She whispers: "We might be evacuated by the end of the year." She writes in secret code, mocking the uniformed men who tear open the envelopes, calling her country's dictator Herr Doktor, or El Jefe. "Bugs Bunny is at it again," she says. "Mr. Potatohead is headed for a *oupcay* if he doesn't watch his *ackbay.*"

I try to think of Africa. I walk up and down the hallway to keep my leg from going to sleep. On the walls I have tacked up pictures and postcards that Camille has sent during the last three years. "The weather reports here say 'hot to very hot,'" Camille writes. "It is the dry season, but worse than usual. There is drought and the crops are failing." Here I see the pictures of the elephant, here is the violently colored sunset, now I'm at the herd of gazelles. And my favorite: Camille, her blonde hair shining, her face tan, smiling wide at the camera, the background a blurry green and yellow.

Dear Camille: Here there is rain. The foundations of the new houses they are building outside of town are filling with water. The doctors say I might need another operation. I move through the rooms of the house quietly, as if someone is sleeping. A habit leftover from when Mother was sick. Dear Camille: Daddy and I watched the Academy Awards. *Schindler's List* won Best Picture.

Did you hear about the Chunnel? Did you hear about Nancy Kerrigan?

At work I'm helping with the children's storytime. There is a little boy named Henry I wish you could meet.

I don't know about my leg. The doctors don't know.

Please, be careful. Be safe.

Be glad, she writes to me. Be well.

People assume, I think, that the car accident we were in as children created the differences between us, made us who we are. I was twelve, Camille was ten. We were squabbling in the backseat. Mother turned to scold us, and didn't see the pickup truck whizzing through the intersection. Camille walked away with one small gash near her eye. There's a thin white scar, crescent moon shape, a fingernail clipping cupping the corner of her eye like a single parentheses. She touches it with the tip of her left ring finger when she's deep in thought, or worried, which isn't often.

I broke my neck. I spent weeks at Children's Mercy in Kansas City. The surgeons grafted some of my hip bone to my neck, and now I walk with a stiff-legged gait—it's the left leg that's the trouble. The accident happened a long time ago but every year there's something new to contend with, some new consequence, some new surgery to consider. Now my legs go numb when I sit for more than ten minutes. The doctors fear I will be paralyzed someday.

"Jenny's the community-minded one," my mother used to say. How hard it must have been on her, and on Camille too—Camille, with her perfect limbs, not just strong but beautiful too, and she did everything—volleyball, track, ballet, swimming. I focused on piano lessons, sewing, volunteer work. "Jenny will do great things one day," my mother said. But it wasn't true, and she knew it.

Camille's country has been heating up, and now it's hot. I haven't had a letter in three weeks. At the public library, where I work, I offer to shelf-read, checking call numbers to be sure the books are in the right place—everybody's least favorite job. At home I don't watch TV; it makes too much noise, and I don't want to miss anything. Even reading is too noisy, some nights. The words in my head, the turning pages. I stand in the hallway, the lights off. I touch the pictures on the wall. Camille, I think. Do you remember? When we were little? How we'd lie in bed together, the same bed, and listen to the quiet? I listen to my own breathing, in, out, in, out. I am waiting for the next thing to happen. But nothing happens. Just the unfolding of days.

"Any word from your sister?" they ask me at work. I shake my head. Two of the circulation pages, high school girls, giggle. They believe I've taken a vow of silence.

On Tuesday mornings I wait to see Henry at story time. He's the one person I speak to. The first time he came he walked right up to me and said, "Did you know that my mother is dead?" "No," I said. "Mine too." He raised his eyebrows and nodded sagely, as if he had already figured this out about us. Now when he comes, with his babysitter, he shouts, "Jenny!" and runs up to hug me. "Careful of her legs," the sitter says, staring. She wears impractical clothes—too short skirts that she keeps tugging on, or stylish but ugly trousers made of velour. She's twenty, and colors her hair. Why?

"He doesn't need to be careful," I tell her. "He can't hurt me." She shrugs.

Henry is four and has a crush on me. I have a crush on his father, whom I have only seen once. His name is Robert. He's a biologist who works for the Tallgrass Prairie Preserve. His library record tells me that he likes travel essays and biographies, and lives only six blocks from me. I memorize the address and sometimes even drive by the house, which is painted cornflower blue, with bright pink and green and yellow Adirondack chairs on the porch. The one time I saw him he was wearing wire-rimmed glasses and a baseball cap and jeans with a hole in one knee. Henry was on his shoulders, and Robert was holding his dangling feet. I don't know when his wife died. He still wears a wedding ring.

Then it happens. The revolution. Camille's country is too small to get much air time on television, but I wait for the images anyway. The faces they show are all black, smiling, laughing. There is a celebration. The President, who has been oppressing the people for decades, has conceded defeat in the first ever election held in his country. He was confident, the journalist in the safari vest reports, that he would win, but he was wrong. President-for-Life no longer. I picture Camille, dancing in the streets with her students, her hair shining in the hot sun. I know one thing: She will come home now. But I try not to think of that. I don't want to jinx anything.

The night of Camille's revolution, Daddy and Elsie come for dinner. I've been cooking all day, Daddy's favorites: roast chicken with a wine herb sauce, mashed turnip, fresh green beans and homemade rolls, twice-baked potatoes, applesauce, a three-layer carrot cake with cream cheese frosting for dessert. I'm too nervous to eat but cooking calms me.

Daddy and Elsie knock once and enter. "So strange, knocking on my own door," Daddy says. "The strangest sensation." He says this every time he comes over.

Elsie kisses me on the cheek. "Smells divine," she says. "No news?"

"Just what they've been saying all day. The elections were uneventful, the dictator was voted out, but the volunteers will be shipped out starting tomorrow, just as a precaution." I'm setting the table: the blue and white woven placemats, tattered at the edges from so many washings, and the hand-carved napkin rings that Camille sent for Christmas, smooth dark wood that I rub lightly against my upper lip, like you do with a baby's velvety head. In the middle of the table is the pot of African violets I bought when Camille left, the thick furry leaves almost obscenely healthy.

"The woman I spoke to at the Embassy this morning was very positive, very optimistic," Daddy says. I hand him the forks and knives and he obediently lays them out. I watch him for a moment, the light on his graying hair, his kind, open face, the way he places each piece of silverware so carefully where it belongs, tapping the handle lightly with his fingertips as if it might drift out of position. I remember when Mother was sick, how he sat in the living room every night by himself, one dim light on and a glass of brandy in his hand. And then Mother died, and Camille graduated and left the country, and it was just me and Daddy here, pretending everything was all right.

In the kitchen, Elsie is bustling. Tonight she wears a pale pink suit like the underside of a seashell, with large fake pearl buttons down the front, encircled in gold. Earrings that match the buttons, shoes and purse dyed to match the suit as if she's in a wedding, pale white hose and a tortoiseshell hairclip holding her swept-up hair. *Dear Camille*, I think. Elsie is looking rich. Like a slice of some cream-filled dessert you can only eat three bites of. Last time you saw her she was just Ricky Wilkes's mother wearing a floppy sunhat and madras shorts from Sears. The world has changed, Camille. Now she owns her own travel agency. Now she's married to our father, and they live in one of those fancy condos off the new golf course, with a swimming pool and concierge service. Concierge service! In this town!

"I'm so excited," Elsie says. "I haven't seen Camille since you and she were just little bitty things. What do you suppose she'll do now, Jenny? Do you think she'll stay put, after all her adventures?"

"I really couldn't say. You never know about Camille."

"I think it's wonderful, that she's been able to go off and see the world at such a young age. I didn't even fly in an airplane until I was twenty-three years old! Of course I've never been to Africa, it never would've occurred to me as a young woman and now, well, there are so many places to go. Belize sounds interesting, doesn't it?" She turns to my father.

"Belize? Oh, yes."

"Jenny, you really ought to take a trip sometime, you know I could get you a good deal. Just pick your location and we'll work something out." Elsie is the one who booked my parents' last cruise together. It was on the cruise that Mother found the lump. Again. For weeks I blamed Elsie for the recurrence—illogical but convenient.

"It's difficult for Jenny to travel," my father says, trying to be helpful.

"Difficult but not impossible! Certainly not! There are all kinds of provisions for the handicapped now." My father and I wince.

"I'll think about it, Elsie. Thank you." Then the timer for the chicken goes off and I'm busy putting food on the table while Elsie screws lids back on jars and fills water glasses noisily with ice and *bustle, bustle* until everything is ready, and we sit down to eat. And the phone rings.

"I'll get it." Elsie bounces up.

"No." I must have sounded sharp enough to convince her the first time because she sits right back down. I know it's Camille.

"Jenny?" she calls to me over the oceans. "How is everything? How is Daddy?"

"We're all fine—but you—are you all right? Are you really coming home?"

"We're getting evacuated tomorrow. We'll fly to Nairobi then to London. I'll call you when I know more. I can't talk now—there's an endless queue for the phone. I'll call from London, okay?"

"Camille!"

"I know. I'll be home soon."

But she isn't.

She travels for a few weeks first—Scandinavia, Scotland, France. She stays with people she knew in the Peace Corps, other volunteers and "ex-pats" as she calls them, and friends of friends, people she doesn't know, people whose phone numbers she keeps in a pocket-sized notebook, people who are accustomed to strangers sleeping on their couches or in sleeping bags on their floors. I try to imagine these apartments, their foreign sinks and toilets, their views, the magazines in other languages piled on coffee tables. But I am only seeing scenes from movies, not real places. Camille sends postcards, which I add to the hallway, but I can't write back; she moves around too much; she doesn't know where she'll be next. I keep busy, preparing the house for her arrival, seeing it through her eyes and suddenly aware of how shabby it has become. I paint, sew new curtains for the kitchen, buy a few colorful cushions for the living room, a new bedspread for Camille's room. "Things are certainly looking bright and shiny around here," Elsie says. Daddy nods in his absent way— change usually upsets him, but there has been so much in the last few years, maybe he is getting used to it.

When it is time to meet Camille's flight, I leave Elsie and Daddy at my house, hanging up the welcome home banner and basting the pork tenderloin. The drive to the Kansas City airport takes two hours, and on the way I have to stop four times to get out and walk. It is a warm day, early June. Wide swaths of prairie are black from controlled burns, but there are patches of new growth, too, green shoots poking out from charred earth.

I have a picture in my head of how our airport reunion will go. I have imagined how she will appear at the gate, I have our conversation all worked out, I have played it over and over in my mind. Like most things, this one doesn't go as I expect.

"Look at me!" Camille wails. "I'm *huge*." Camille isn't huge. But she is, without a doubt, pregnant.

She throws her arms around my neck. She smells of air travel and peppermint gum, and looks as if there is a light inside her, spilling out in places, like her eyes and skin and teeth. I don't mean a pregnancy glow—this is just Camille. "I would've had to come home anyway," she says, "even without the evacuation." We're walking through the terminal, and she has her arm around me.

"I just can't believe this. I mean, Camille—a baby!"

"Let's not talk about it now. Here, here's the baggage claim for my flight. I just have the one bag," and then she starts talking about London, and someone she saw at JFK, a friend she hasn't seen in ages, he was just returning from a Fulbright in Italy, and I know from the way she speaks that he is an old lover, and seeing him again has presented her with yet another option, as viable as any other, but I'm only half listening. We pick up her duffel bag and on the way to the car she hooks her arm in mine and kisses my cheek. "I'm so happy to see you." And I bask in her light, knowing it is only a matter of time before she takes it away again.

In the car we make small talk until we get to the interstate. I can feel her looking and looking at everything, as she always has, her eyes wide open, her lips almost smiling.

"So Camille," I say. "Whose is it?"

She keeps looking at the scenery as if I haven't spoken. "Probably Jo Jo. Very sweet, gentle man. West Indian. You'd like him."

I'm trying to digest that "probably." "Does he know? About the baby?"

"The thing is, honey." She glances at me, then back out the window. "He's married, is the thing."

I try to put it all together. My sister is pregnant with another woman's husband's baby. West Indian. Gentle and sweet. Is that how his wife would describe him? Is she Camille's friend, too?

And why didn't she write me this?

We talk about other things, Daddy, and the people she stayed with in Europe, and after a while I pull into a rest stop to stretch my legs. Camille gets out too. I lean against a picnic table while she massages my back for a few minutes. Her fingers have always known where to go and where not to go, and they move around my spine, cautious at first, remembering.

"I've got some offers, to do some consulting work," she says. "For some international programs. A lot of it's just going through reports, making recommendations. Stuff I could do anywhere. So I think I might stay with you, if it's okay, until . . . I deliver." She talks about some fundraising projects for the school where she worked. The Peace Corps also wants to hire her to train other teachers, and she could use the time before the baby comes to organize her materials. She'll need a room to set up as an office. I assure her I have loads of space. I begin to feel happy.

Then she takes me by the shoulders, turns me to face her so that we are almost nose to nose, the two of us standing there under the big sky, cars and eighteen wheelers whooshing by. "And Jenny," she says. "I don't know what I'm going to do about the baby. Okay?" She speaks slowly and clearly, as if I'm dimwitted or deaf—a lip reader. "I'm just telling you, straight out. I haven't decided to keep it or give it up for adoption or anything."

"Okay," I say. "I understand." But now that I know she is going to stay, I am already making plans. I'll turn Mother's old room into a nursery. I'll make curtains, a yellow and white check, and maybe put up some wallpaper. We walk back to the car holding hands, and I don't acknowledge to Camille the nagging desire I've been feeling ever since seeing her come off that plane, belly-first. But it is clear to me now.

I want that baby.

Camille brings life into the house. She fills the spare room downstairs with a computer, a fax machine, eventually even a photocopier that she buys cheap at an auction somewhere. One of her projects involves organizing shipments of school supplies to villages like hers. She speaks at local churches and the community college and at the library too, and pretty soon people are streaming in and out of the house at all hours, packing up boxes and preparing mailings and faxing who knows what to the outside world. Some people are connectors, my mother used to say. That's Camille. With every passing week of summer Camille grows larger, and I sew her some maternity dresses, sleeveless with big pockets where she can keep the memo pad she's constantly scribbling in, and the mobile phone she walks around talking into. I set her up with an obstetrician that a friend recommends, and she dutifully keeps her appointments, though she dismisses the idea of Lamaze.

I'm getting into the habit of waking up early, for the quiet. I start a pot of chili or stew on the stove, leave it out with some bowls and napkins. By bedtime it's gone. Lately I feel my mother's presence with me in the early mornings, sitting at the kitchen table studying her nails, humming. I figure she's back because Camille's home, and she knows something interesting will happen now. It's such a strong feeling I stop chopping the onions or browning the meat, and stare hard at the chair that was hers, but nothing happens.

At night I read books on childbirth and childcare, and I work on the nursery—making curtains and a baby quilt with blue and pink and yellow hearts in the squares. Camille doesn't know. She only comes upstairs at bedtime. Downstairs, she stays on the phone till all hours. Pregnancy insomnia, she says. I lay out patterns and cut fabric, listening to Camille's voice rising and falling, listening to the tones that say Camille is concerned, Camille is helping, Camille is joyous. I listen to her laugh. And I'm happy: my sister home, a baby on the way; the sewing machine thrumming; my hands making useful and beautiful things, the first things that this baby will know. Purpose plants itself inside me, taking root and spreading into everything I do. I hum and smile and go to bed tired, my hip and leg aching but I don't mind anymore. It's like someone else's leg. I'm sorry about it, but really, it doesn't seem to have much to do with me.

Then, a July evening, almost nine but still light out. I'm upstairs, finishing a bumper for the crib. It matches the curtains and the quilt and I'm feeling pleased with myself, with how everything is coming together, when the door opens. "Jen, I was wondering where—" Camille stops when she sees Mother's room. I haven't put the crib together yet but it's there, in its box, leaning against the changing table I bought at a yard sale. And there is of course the wallpaper border with hearts and lambs and teddy bears, and then there's me, sitting at the sewing machine, looking caught.

In all my preparations I haven't anticipated or planned for this moment. I kept thinking we might skip this part, just get to the baby-part and then wouldn't it be a nice surprise, to see how I'd gotten everything ready?

Camille sucks in her breath. She begins, slowly, walking around the room, touching things as if to see whether they're real—the stack of Pampers, the box of wipes, the almost-finished quilt folded on top of the dresser. She opens up one of the drawers and sees the stack of onesies I've bought, still in their plastic wrappers. Her back is to me so I can't see her expression, but I'm pretty sure I know what it is.

"I just thought—" but I don't know what to say.

She turns, one hand on her belly. "You just thought, what?"

"Camille," I plead. She's dabbing at the crescent scar with her ring finger. Then she crosses her arms on top of the shelf that is her stomach. Her voice is quiet and even. "You realize, don't you, that if I'd been in the States when this happened, I would have had an abortion. I mean, without a second thought. You get that, don't you?"

I nod. I stand up to get my circulation going, then sit down again. A fax beeps downstairs; the phone rings, but Camille lets the answering machine pick up. She's watching me this whole time. "I'm going back to Africa. I'm leaving after the baby's born."

"And—"

"That's all I have to know right now."

And then something happens to me. I'm so angry my leg is trembling. "Camille, this is a baby you're talking about. And if you're giving it up for adoption then you'd better see a lawyer or an agency or something. And if you're keeping it then you'd better think about how you're going to travel to a disease-infested country with a newborn, and you'd better let me know one way or the other before this baby is born."

"I don't have to let you know anything. This is not your problem, Jenny. This is not your pregnancy. I knew you were going to take over as soon as I got here. I knew it. God! If I'd had *anyplace* else to go." She shakes herself as if something's gotten on her clothes and she wants it off. Then she turns around at the door. "You're right. I'm in major denial here. I grant you that. But you, my dear sister"—she indicates the room with a nod of her head—"you are living in fantasy land."

And then she's out the door.

I look down at the bumper with the hearts on it. I look at the wallpaper, the box with the crib, a picture on the box of a baby in the crib, the way it should look once you have everything assembled. I rip out the stitches in the fabric I've been sewing, and leave it in a heap on the floor.

As usual, Daddy and Elsie try to get information out of me. "You're living with her," Elsie says. "You must know something."

"All I know is, she's going back to Africa as soon as she can."

"With the baby?" Elsie wants to give Camille a baby shower, but I've convinced her to wait.

"How should I know? I suppose she'll figure that out when she has the baby."

I stay away from the house as much as possible. Our fight

hangs over everything and I can't walk through the rooms without feeling it, like something damp clinging to my skin. The two of us are living together in the same house where we were babies and children and teenagers. But we hardly see each other. When we do, we are polite, formal. "Good morning," we say. Or, "How is work going?" Fine thank you. Everything is going well. One night I get out Camille's letters and read them by number, not date. She numbered them because often they arrived out of order, some letters inexplicably hung up for weeks while others arrived in the usual fifteen days. I read them and listen to the voice that used to tell me things. I look for clues to what was really going on, I calculate dates, I comb the letters for references to Jo Jo, anything. But it turns out she wasn't talking to me as much as I thought.

The nursery door stays closed. I don't want to go in there anymore. I refuse to think about the baby so instead it comes to me at night, in dreams so lacking in subtlety they embarrass me. Sometimes the baby is sick. No one wants it. It's been left in my basket of gardening tools. When I discover it, it's too late. I bury the gray body in my flowerbed, shoveling the dirt with a cracked wooden spoon.

Just when I think we might go on like this forever, it's an August night, two in the morning, and Camille comes into my bedroom. When we were little she often came into my room in the middle of the night to sleep with me, and for a moment I am confused about when this is happening. She whispers, as if we aren't the only people in the house, her voice taut and amazed.

"Jenny! My water broke!"

"What? Are you sure?" I'm whispering too.

"Either that or I just wet the bed." We start giggling, and it's us again, giggling in my bed. I finally have the presence of mind to turn on the light. Her face startles me. "Camille, are you all right?"

"I don't want to do this. I don't want to." Then I'm holding her and talking to her as if she's worried about a test the next day, or a swim meet. "Honey, you're going to do great." I hug her and kiss her cheek and note the panic in her eyes. "Here, you rest right here"—I lay her on my bed—"while I call the hospital. Do you have a bag packed?" She shakes her head no. "Have the contractions started?" She shakes her head again. I press her hands and put on a T-shirt and a pair of jeans and tennis shoes. Downstairs I find the number to the hospital, which I've written in black magic marker on the inside of the phone book. I walk as fast as I can, back upstairs to Camille's room. The duffel bag is on the floor of the closet. I open her dresser, the clothes thrown in there without, apparently, having been folded, and gather some shirts and shorts and underwear and throw them into the bag, trying to remember what the books say to bring. All I can come up with is lip balm, and by the time I find a tube of Carmex in the bathroom cabinet, and get back to my room, Camille is sitting on the edge of the bed, hands on her knees, staring at the floor as if it's about to open up and swallow her. She's breathing like she's gone to those classes after all.

"They've started," she says.

Camille does childbirth the way she does everything else. She dispenses quickly with her fear, then gets down to business. The nurses are astonished—a first baby and only two hours' labor. It is almost unheard of.

When it comes, it's a girl. Camille looks at her, the light eyes and skin, and says, her voice even, "I guess it was Ken's after all." The nurses exchange glances, then begin their poking and sponging and weighing. They wrap the baby in a receiving blanket and hand her to Camille. She takes her without hesitating. I start to put my hand out, to say no, but Camille unties her gown and puts the baby right to her breast as if she's done this before. The books all say that sometimes the newborn doesn't latch on right away, that a new mother must be schooled in the art of breastfeeding. But this mother and baby are two animals burrowing down in their nest, requiring only each other. I feel a tugging inside me, almost a physical tearing, and I have to sit down. This is when Camille looks at me, really sees me for the first time since I checked her into the hospital.

"Isabel," she says. I nod, because I already know this. Our mother's name.

My sister sends me letters from England.

They manage to be careful and breezy at the same time. Camille has a new job in London; she left right after Isabel was born. That was always her plan, as it turns out—not Africa. Ken, Isabel's father, has moved from Nairobi. They did a paternity test to make sure. He takes care of the baby while Camille works. I've talked to him on the phone, once. He sounds nice.

"We're trying it out anyway," Camille writes. "I'll keep you posted."

I still write her letters, but not in my head anymore.

Last week I called the doctor's office. I told his nurse to go ahead and schedule the surgery. "Tell him, sometime before Christmas. Tell him I'm ready." I'm not sure I am ready. But I could have a leg that works almost the way it should. It seems worth the gamble.

At home, the door of the nursery stays closed.

At work, the children's librarian is taking a leave of absence—her husband is ill—and I'm substituting for an unspecified period of time. I love this job. I have already set up after-school reading clubs and changed all the bulletin board displays. Henry, who has been staying with his grandparents in Colorado all summer, arrives for a Saturday morning story time, and approaches me shyly. Before long, though, he is giving me the full report on his first week in kindergarten. He looks like a different boy! His hair is lighter, and there are freckles on his nose. He's two inches taller, at least. And he's taken on a new swagger, which I admire.

"I went hiking with my dad up a mountain," he tells me. "There was a hailstorm and we had to make a tent out of our ponchos. And I saw a *porcupine*." At the end of story time, Henry's father shows up. Whatever I once imagined about this person so many months ago no longer pertains. I introduce myself, put out my hand, which he takes.

"Henry's a huge fan of yours."

I smile. "The feeling is mutual."

We keep talking. At this moment I don't have any feeling about Robert one way or the other. He's just a person I'm talking to, in the children's library, with noisy kids running around. We talk as if we already know each other, as if we're friends of friends, people who have met before at a social event, which, in this town, is always a possibility. He asks about books he should check out for Henry. I ask about their summer vacation. "I've never been to Colorado," I admit. He says I should go sometime. He says the fly-fishing is terrific, and the mountain air a relief from the Kansas summers. I imagine a stream, and a tent pitched under aspens. Sleeping bag, backpack, camp stove, flashlight, everything I need, right there.

Henry starts pulling at his father, nagging him to go home.

"Do you want to get coffee sometime?" he asks me. "Or lunch? Henry and I usually go to the mall for Chinese on Sundays."

"Sure," I say. "Lunch would be great."

We leave it at that—maybe next week, maybe the week after. Or maybe not. I'm trying to be realistic.

That Reminds Me

I'm in the kitchen, slicing carrots for minestrone, and the way I chop them—on the diagonal, so that the carrot becomes a neat row of oval discs—reminds me of Gerry, who used to watch me prepare carrots this way (I loved cooking for him). He took to slicing carrots this way, too, and he said to me one day, Now whenever I slice carrots on the diagonal, I'll think of you. And I knew he meant, after we're over. He meant, when we're no longer together and he's doing the carrots for someone else's salad or stew— for the new woman in his life or the mother of his as yet unborn children—as he places the knife on the carrot at an angle and presses down to produce that pretty oval shape, the slicing of the carrot will bring me back to him, and in this way he will not forget me, or if he does, for a period of days or weeks, there will always be a time when he will once again slice a carrot on the diagonal, or start to do it the old way and then switch to the diagonal way, and I will come back to him. After we're done with each other, these things will remind him of me. Carrots and the particular way I have of laying the napkin on the placemat or salting my food (quick, adamant shakes). Other things too.

When he said, and implied, all this, I laughed, and said, That's funny, because when I slice carrots this way, I think of Rick (my boyfriend before Gerry). I learned to slice carrots on the diagonal from him, so whenever I slice carrots I remember Rick's Chinese cleaver rocking back and forth against the wooden board—he'd worked as a cook before going to law school—and the way he tied a bandana kamikaze style around his forehead to keep the hair out of his eyes, and how while he cooked he played Robert Cray or the Fabulous Thunderbirds on the stereo, loud, and he danced, and he danced with me, swinging me around the kitchen while vegetables simmered in butter, and we drank while waiting for the food to be ready, gin in the summer and scotch in the winter, and I remember how I loved the day when he'd bring home the limes and the tonic and announce, Summer is here. So now, I told Gerry, whenever I slice carrots, I'll think of you thinking of me, and I'll think of Rick, and I'll also just be in my kitchen of the moment slicing carrots. And he laughed too and said now he'd have to think of me, and Rick, who is someone he used to be friends with, and he'd also have to think of me thinking of Rick *and* thinking of him.

But I wonder now if he does. If he remembers what I said about Rick teaching me the whole carrot on the diagonal thing, if he remembers that while I was chopping carrots to make dinner for him, I was thinking of Rick, and not of him. I wonder if he thinks about the carrots at all, or even chops carrots, or when he does maybe he just slices them in the old way, the way he used to before we met. Sometimes I do the carrots that way too, just so I can avoid this whole chain of thoughts, though of course I can't really avoid it because thinking about avoiding it is really the same as thinking about it, and everything is like this, things within things, one leading to the next. The carrots are just the beginning.

Anniversary

Dixie cup, ice pick, string, thumbtacks. Thomas gauging the drops of water, me lying on the green shag rug in my room. "Keep your eyes open," he instructed. "No cheating." Comic book SPLATs dropped on my forehead then rolled down my temples and into my ears. Were prisoners really tortured this way in China? And what secrets did the water make them tell? Eventually I realized that my brother had abandoned his post outside my door— he was downstairs eating Ring Dings or riding his Sting Ray in the driveway, and the game, though I was still in it, was over.

Some years, I wake up and don't remember right away. I check the calendar for appointments or open up the morning paper, and I see the date. Oh—it's today. And then it's there as I pour cereal for the children, wait for the lawyer to return my call, throw in a load of laundry, search for the swimming goggles. It's there and I try to look just past it or else I try to remember things, but it's the same old stuff, like the stagnant breath of vase water when you dump the dead flowers.

* * *

Thomas's index fingers, nails bitten down past anything, drumming hard against the dinner table. He used to sit hunched over, his head nodding, keeping time to imagined music. He wanted to be a rock star; he had an electric guitar and amp in his room, and he taught himself to play, sort of. His hair was parted way over to one side, 70s style, so that the long bangs fell across half his face. He used English Leather cologne, like the fifth grade substitute teacher. My real teacher, a woman I loved, was recovering from back surgery, and missed almost the entire school year. The substitute was a lanky man with a goofy freckled face and a bushy moustache. One morning he taught photosynthesis with his fly down. The winking white briefs left me and Kim Mahoney—the only other kid in class whose parents were separated—in fits of horrified giggles.

Here we are around the table, me, edgy, waiting for cues, wondering what might happen next, only wanting everything to be normal; our mother lovely and thin and sad, child-size portions on her plate, a dozen strands of spaghetti, a tablespoon of meat sauce; our father's chair empty—maybe that was the year he lived with the photography student in California, or maybe it was a different year; Thomas with his fringe jacket on, the suede reeking of cigarette smoke. Everything about him said, As soon as we're done here, I'm out the door.

When we were first together, Aaron used to ask me about Thomas. I told him what I remembered: the hair, the coat, the smirk. How he'd put his dishes in the sink, then get in his VW, gun the engine, and go.

It is the morning of the day I anticipate even though nothing is going to happen on this day. No cards or flowers or phone calls. This year it means getting the children up early for my four-year-old's swimming lessons. The lessons began yesterday and last for two weeks. I signed him up before I knew how my marriage was going to turn out. Or at least, when I was still hopeful. When was that? April. Is that possible? That I was optimistic enough just two months ago to commit to swimming lessons? Having paid the money I can no longer afford, I am taking Danny to the city pool even though I know we are doomed. Yesterday, he "bumped" his elbow. He hurts his arm like this, or pretends to, when he wants to get out of doing something. It's always his arm, so Arm has become a code, a symbol for something else.

I know he misses his father. But a hundred and twenty-five dollars! No refunds!

Today I've managed so far—and in moments of humor I'm able to see myself as a superwoman, an *überfrau*—to get everyone into bathing suits, which has meant locating exactly where the suits were peeled off and deposited yesterday (one at the bottom of the basement stairs, one in the pop-up tent in Danny's room). I have packed sippy cups of apple juice and boxes of animal crackers. I have remembered towels, diapers, swim diapers, sunscreen, sunglasses, sunhats, clothes, pool toys, wipes. I have found Danny's goggles on the shelf above the washing machine. I have put truculent feet into sandals and buckled everyone into carseats. We're late, always late. By the time we reach the pool the lessons have already begun.

"I don't want to go," Danny says. He is biting the insides of his cheeks.

From here I can see the other, more organized mothers already perched on benches or wading in the kiddie pool with their younger children. I want to put the car in reverse, and watch Danny's secret relief in the rearview mirror.

"You'll have your goggles today, honey. You'll do great." I unbuckle everyone, carry Jessica in her carseat carrier in one hand, the stuffed totebag in the other. Danny is watching his group, the Little Flippers. They are already in the water with their teacher, a busty, tanned teenager named Gretchen. Danny shakes his head but lets me lead him to the pool. "I'll be right over here, in the kiddie pool, okay?"

Gretchen cajoles Danny into the water, and I want to say, no, not like that, he hates teasing—but I have to stay focused. The baby fusses. Audrey skirts around the edges of a new tantrum, pulling at my terry cloth cover-up. I blow up the inflatable dragon inner tube, change her into a swim diaper, lift Jessica from the carrier. Under my cover-up is the maternity bathing suit because I'm still too fat for the regular one. Three kids in three and a half years. It can be done, but I don't recommend it, especially if your husband has other plans. I dangle Jessica's feet in the water. If I turn around, I can see the Little Flippers from here, but I don't turn yet.

The boys in our neighborhood built a shack out of plywood and sheets of tin. The shack stood in the field that separated our old farmhouse from the housing development behind us. These streets had inane names—Sherwood Forest, Robin Hood Lane, Little John Circle. Later the field was sold to a building contractor who added more split-levels; I babysat children in those houses. But while Thomas was a teenager and still living at home, the field belonged to the boys. They smoked cigarettes and drank pilfered Millers, hung up Playboy centerfolds from their fathers' discarded piles, played cards, hung out.

I was allowed in the shack once. I can't imagine what series of circumstances led to this lapse, but I do remember the old army-green sleeping bags with their hunting-dog-print liners, the hubcap ashtray, the empty cans and bottles scattered in the tall grass like mushrooms after rain. Thomas thought it was funny when T.J. Bori, one of the older neighborhood kids, started swearing in front of me. "Goddamn it," he said, then studied my face for a reaction. "There's nothing wrong with saying goddamn," he explained. "You're just asking *God* to *damn* something." I wasn't shocked or offended. Neither "God" nor "damn" meant much to me. I just shrugged. The boys laughed anyway, as if I had responded the way they wanted.

Thomas had a girlfriend named Lynne. I liked Lynne because she had given me a peace sign medallion on a rawhide string for Christmas, and it was the coolest thing I owned. Sometimes Thomas hung out at a church near our house because Lynne went to the Youth Group there. My mother and I saw the two of them once, as we drove by. They were sitting on the church lawn, Thomas's suede arm around the long-haired Lynne's shoulders. They were laughing, stoned out of their minds, though I didn't understand this until later.

In summer school after his seventh grade year, the other kids locked Thomas in a storage closet. He spent the morning there. Where were the teachers back then? What did he think about, sitting in the closet in the dark, breathing in the pulpy paper and boxes of chalk? A guidance counselor in ninth grade said, "Thomas will make a fine garbage man some day." This, in front of the whole class. Once I found an essay he had written crumpled in the trash. The assignment was a self-portrait. "I see a boy with brown eyes and brown hair," he wrote in scrawling pencil. "He is a lonely boy who doesn't have many friends." In the middle of his sophomore year, grades falling, drug use escalating, my mother was advised to send him to boarding school. The experts believed this was the best thing.

Danny won't put his face in the water. The other Flippers are doing their bobs, popping in and out of the water like corks. The mothers of these children, cheerful women with permed hair and pedicures, are the good mothers. They are married to the fathers of these children and they have chosen well— their men aren't the leaving kind. Since the birth of their little flippers, they've enrolled them in a series of self-improvement classes, beginning with parent-infant swimming lessons and moving up to parent-tot. Now the children are fish, little fish who also play Suzuki violin, leap across the high school auditorium every spring in hundred-dollar costumes, kick a soccer ball with alarming enthusiasm, perform somersaults on gymnastic mats, know the French words for *good night* and *cat*.

This is what Danny is up against: children who have been raised by professionals. His mother, on the other hand, is given to clandestine weeping in the grocery store. She has been known to abandon her cart altogether.

The women's voices rise and fall as they talk to their toddlers but I can't make out the words. Where was I, what was I doing, when these women were dunking their newborns underwater like Baptists at the river? Hoping Aaron wouldn't leave me, which he has now done. Waiting for my milk to come in, umbilical cords to fall off, nipples to heal, babies to sleep. So much of it is about fatigue. Do you have the energy to live your life, or don't you? It isn't because fathers leave or mothers can't reach across a dinner table to still those drumming fingers and say, Where? Where are you going? It's just whether or not you can keep your own head above water.

Audrey, who at two already seems filled with the rage of the disenfranchised, is at this moment floating in her inner tube, murmuring about birds, her eyes closed like a blues singer. Jessica has fallen asleep in the carrier, her mouth still working the pacifier. From here I can see the playground where I have spent hundreds of bored hours. Three teenage girls swing high. One of them has a loud laugh. A woman reads a magazine on a bench, her sons—twins—crashing their yellow Tonka trucks into each other. The clouds are almost absurd in their perfect white puffiness, drifting across large skies. Audrey fills and dumps an old Cool Whip container. Jessica sleeps. I need to look over at Danny. I know he needs me to.

I dreamed that Thomas came to pick me up in his red VW bug. He looked straight ahead as I got into the car. He was wearing his fringe coat, his hair hiding one eye. Right away I could see that something was wrong. Something in his face. He was dead, of course. He was driving, but he was dead. He let me get out of the car, but not before he had turned that distorted, pale face to me, as if to say, See? Do you get it now? He drove off, calling out Bye! Bye! in this jaunty way that didn't go with what had come before. I woke up to the car backfiring, small explosive bursts.

I turn. Danny is watching me. He's been watching me this whole time. His hair ruffles in the breeze, his brown eyes are glossy and beseeching even through the goggles. He holds his arm against his bony chest. We're maybe twenty yards from each other. I call out to him, "Okay, Danny. I'm coming." I am trying to sound like someone who can get through the day. He doesn't care if I'm mad or crazy, as long as he is freed from the terrible water, from the tyranny of his peers with their sleek bobbing heads. Gretchen shrugs as he climbs the ladder.

It's just the day that it is, always this day.

"Come back and try again tomorrow, Dan the man," Gretchen says, for my benefit. I wrap a towel around his fragile shoulders, and even Audrey gets out of the pool fast when I ask her to in this voice. I avoid the stares of the other mothers. It's a small town, I'll have to face them somewhere—the store, the park, in line at McDonald's—but not now.

"Danny's so much like me," Aaron said once. We had just come from Danny's preschool Christmas program, where he stood on the stage like someone accused, working his mouth painfully but not singing the words. "It kills me, watching him, how careful and wary he is."

"He'll grow out of it," I told him. "You did."

"I just love him so much."

Then don't leave, I wanted to say. But I didn't say anything.

97

"If you can't say no to that man, you should walk away," my girlfriend told me when Aaron and I were first together. She could see how I'd gone overboard. How he'd call, drunk, at three in the morning, and I'd let him come over to have sex even though I had to get up for work two hours later. Of course I did. "Why can't he ever call during the day?" she said. She called him the Vampire. But she knew how it was, how she could lecture me all night over martinis and Marlboro Lights and it wouldn't do any good.

I feel as if I have stepped out of that dark old bar and into this June sun, squinting and headachy. I lug the baby in her carrier (awake now, and crying), the pool bag, the dragon, struggle with everything into the parking lot. When it's time to cross, Audrey reaches up for Danny's hand, and he takes it.

When you play Cheeseit you wait for the cars, wait until the last minute, then you yell *Cheeseit!* and run behind the pine trees, heart racing, you can't let them see you and you're clutching your money, waiting for the ice cream truck, sometimes pitching nickels under the tires of passing cars then running into the street afterwards to hunt for the shining coins. The tar on the road gets soft in the heat and you dig at it with a stick, carve your initials. When you play Army, the boys get the machine guns but they let you be the nurse. You have your nurse kit from your birthday, the white hat with the red plus sign on the front. You dart across the back yard avoiding land mines, tending to the wounded. Sometimes T.J. Bori plays even though he is too old for this game, and you always remember as you bandage up his wounds with toilet paper how he took you into the upstairs bathroom that time. He needed to, he said, because he was going to be a doctor. T.J. didn't hurt you. In fact, later you think about this scene a lot. On the battlefield, however, you know that he is the one who throws the peach pit grenade too hard at your brother's face and now in terms of nursing you are way over your head and run to get your mother, and then there's the trip to the hospital and the yellow stuff coming out of Thomas's eye and the glasses with the steel-gray frames that he had to wear after that; *partially blind in one eye* was something else they said about him now. Later everyone was glad about the blind eye, because of the draft. T.J., with his immigrant parents and their failed greenhouse business, enlisted. Three years after throwing the dried peach pit at Thomas, he was gone. Girls at school carried green army bags for purses and drew peace signs on them with ballpoint pens. They wore their brothers' dog tags. You could order special bracelets from magazines with the names of guys who were MIA. I wanted Thomas's name on a chain around my neck.

The phone is ringing when we get home from the pool. It's Aaron. "Just wanted to check on you," he says. He's always been nice about Thomas. He's in Spain, and I wonder how he got so far away so fast. He talks to each of the children, even Jessica, who coos back obligingly. He'll be back, he says, before the twenty-seventh. Our court date. As if I need to be reminded.

He shouldn't have called. He thinks he's being sensitive and good. The good soon-to-be-ex-husband, still concerned about his wife's well-being. He grew up an only child, and you can tell.

I take off the children's swimsuits, nurse the baby, put her in her swing. Give Audrey a grape jelly sandwich, no crusts. Danny curls up on my lap, still holding his arm. After a while I get him lunch and put on *Abbey Road*, my one ritual.

I see my brother again, as I have seen him all day, collapsed on the kitchen floor, black T-shirt, Levis, bare feet. He was eighteen. He had just graduated from high school. Ruptured brain aneurysm: Even if I had found him right away, instead of hours later, nothing, the doctors promised me, could have been done.

* * *

I remember the fight Thomas and I had, when I hurled this album (his LP, not the CD I am playing now) down the stairs then ran into my room and locked the door, certain I would be killed. *Bang bang Maxwell's silver hammer came down upon her head* . . . He liked scaring me, when we were alone in the house. He went outside and made scratchy noises at the door. He appeared suddenly at the living room window, making terrible faces. I waited and waited, knowing he was about to pop up, shrieking when he did. My screams delighted him. That's why I threw the album down the stairs.

I pick up Danny. His legs wrap around me and we dance around the living room. He knows these songs. We sing them together: "Oh! Darling" and "Here Comes the Sun" and "She Came In Through the Bathroom Window."

Someday, of course, he will leave me. I'll think he's upstairs, doing his homework, but he'll be sneaking out the back door, holding a twenty-dollar bill from my wallet, or lighting a cigarette. The sounds will be familiar: a car pulling out of the driveway, tires on a wet street, the gunning of the engine. I'll listen for a moment, then turn back to my new lover, or the dishes in the sink.

But right now I kiss him on the neck, to make him laugh. I kiss him many times. I breathe him in: warm skin, hair, breath.

Falling Up

Elliot's wife Rita was prone to fits of rage, seemingly random, and exacerbated by any expression of concern, so that he had learned to embody a certain blankness in her angry presence and waited, in that blankness, for her sweet, conciliatory self to reappear, which it did—though sometimes hours, even days, later. He imagined himself the waters of a calm lake, or a rock on the bottom of that lake, sitting in thick silt, in the deep still cold. He realized he'd spent a lot of years, if you added it all up together, as a rock on the bottom of a lake, but Elliot shrugged off these observations just as he shrugged off close line calls in his weekly doubles match or dips in the market or dead fish in his saltwater tank or any of the many other things beyond his control.

Still, it wasn't easy to live with someone who chafed and strained against—as she said—the role she'd been forced into, through marriage, through childbearing, at the particular point in history that decreed her not only mother but housekeeper and caretaker and chef and laundress and accountant and chauffeur—Rita could go on rather impressively with this list. Her ranting pained Elliot, for he saw these roles as choices she had once willingly made, and the suggestion of force implicated him in ways that made him feel powerless and mean.

Time had helped. She was nicer than she used to be. Their four children—in a matter of minutes, it seemed now, though he remembered some long days—grew up. The two older boys attended the state university a few hours' drive from home, graduated, got jobs, married. Elliot hoped there would soon be grandchildren. The third child, the only girl, chose a school in California, two thousand miles away. She had recently declared she would never marry.

When the last child left for college, Rita proclaimed herself done. They spent the day loading up the car, driving, unloading, going up and down two flights of stairs (his dorm room on the same floor as his brothers' had been, lending a jarring déjà vu to the occasion). This son didn't need them to hang around—he'd seen it all before. Elliot and Rita were back in the car well before dark.

"I'm officially retired, Elliot. Effective today. No more cooking or cleaning, no more confirming your dental appointments or buying Christmas presents for your sisters." She was not spiteful; she was matter-of-fact. She explained, sitting there with the canvas tote she used as a purse and book bag on her lap, how he could cook his own meals if he liked, or go out, or sometimes if she wasn't too busy they could plan to go to a restaurant together, but she had a lot to do and he would have to check with her a few days in advance. She would do her own laundry, or more likely send it out, and he could do his, but he shouldn't expect her to fold or put away his clothes anymore. Ever. Same with the house. She had hired a girl to clean the bathrooms once a week, and vacuum, and a boy to manage the yard; if there was anything else he wanted to have done, he would have to do it.

Elliot felt panic rising in him. Not that he didn't think he could manage—he knew he could—but he worried that the calmness veiled the old hostility, that there would be other, hidden prices to pay.

That night, Rita skipped dinner to attend her T'ai Chi class. She would pick up a salad on the way home. He stood at the living room window and watched her car leave the driveway. In the kitchen he surveyed the contents of the cabinet and refrigerator, and decided on tomato soup and a grilled ham and cheese sandwich. He waited to see what it was he felt. The house was quiet. Outside in the late summer evening a line of starlings lifted from the telephone wire and into the sky, like confetti falling up instead of down. The chairs around the table that had recently held his small, then large, children, and his complicated wife, sat empty. He picked up his spoon, dipped it into the soup. He remembered the many nights around this table, the grim setting forth of platters of meat, bowls of steaming vegetables, sometimes overcooked, sometimes almost raw, the basket of rolls provided grudgingly since Rita eschewed bread; he remembered his obligatory compliments, how he had to offer up different adjectives for chicken, green beans, pork chops, baked potato, to demonstrate his appreciativeness; he remembered Rita responding with a near-grunt or half-smile, acknowledging his attempts but disdaining them at the same time—still, a better reaction than had he said nothing at all.

Elliot should have encouraged her to take that retail job she wanted, a dozen years ago. She had interviewed secretly, to surprise him she said, and was offered the job. The children were all, finally, in school. The job was at an arts and crafts store. She was a knitter and scrapbooker back then. But the position required some weekend and evening hours, and the money would hardly be worth her time, and he said she should think about it, he said maybe if she really wanted a job she could find something part-time during the school day, he said—he told her, No. He knew, now, that he had made a mistake. He hadn't *forbidden* her. Of course not! But he questioned her about how many evenings, how many weekends, and what about the times he had to stay late at work, he hated to think of the children eating dinner alone, and none of the other partners had wives who worked—

He dipped his spoon into the tomato soup. He had used milk instead of water, the variation suggested on the can. The soup was good. He took another spoonful. The soup wasn't just good—the soup was sublime. Elliot closed his eyes, encountered the tangy sweetness of tomato as it met his lips, his tongue. He took a bite of sandwich, he chewed, he slurped his soup. He made a point of slurping. He poured himself a glass of wine, which he almost never did, and he swirled the wine in its glass, admiring the legs, though he knew this gesture was more affectation than useful evaluative tool. *Les larmes du vin*—tears of wine. He put on a record— they still had their old turntable set up in the living room— spending a long time choosing the exact album he wanted to hear. The music reminded him of Nadine, his college girlfriend, who broke off their engagement the day before their graduation. "She was too pretty for you," Rita said, which was true. Nadine had married someone else, divorced, remarried. Elliot didn't know the husbands.

He did the dishes, fed his fish, and sat on the couch to read. He had not pictured this first night of the empty house like this, not at all. What had he expected? Dinner, a movie, a walk downtown. Unlike Rita, he had no plans to retire soon. He wouldn't know what to do without his work, the order it provided.

When Rita came home, Elliot was dozing, a book in his lap. She didn't bother waking him. Her new life had begun with a briskness that satisfied her. The calendar in the kitchen was filled with her small print: book group, pottery, conversational Japanese, creative writing, financial planning for women over fifty. She wasn't sure how Elliot would manage. But she was done worrying about Elliot. Still, she noted the empty soup can in the trash, the dishes drying amateurishly on a hand towel, the wine glass (he'd had *wine* with his Campbell's?) cloudy with condensation because he hadn't tipped it properly to allow the air to circulate. She started to shift the glass to the correct position, then shook her head and put it back on the towel.

She turned off the lights. She felt as if she were spying on an acquaintance, someone she had imagined living a very different kind of life from the one she now observed. Maybe she was being a little *too* brisk. She stood in front of his chair, watching him sleep. The window behind him was open, and a breeze lifted his thinning hair up, then down again.

He knew she was there, of course. He had heard the automatic garage door open, then close, her workout bag drop to the floor, her keys in the wooden bowl. He felt her standing there now. He wondered what her face looked like. He kept his eyes closed.

"Hello," he said.

Mine

Cars, buildings, trees, parking meters, telephone poles—everything looked more solid tonight, sharper and weightier, as if the world had gained an added dimension while Marla convalesced. She'd spent the week lying in bed with a bad cold, thinking too much about her son, whom she considered missing (though he wasn't *technically* missing). The air was raw and cold, an evening in early March. She wore her splendid black wool cape and a velvet purple and red scarf, and leaned on Griffin's arm as they entered the restaurant. Griffin was her second husband; David was her first. She still thought of him as hers, though he was remarried, too.

The husbands shared a birthday. The four of them celebrated together, a tradition that only seemed strange to other people. Marla liked sitting at a small table with the two husbands. She even liked Sloane, David's wife, as unlikely as that seemed. Sloane was Marla's opposite in every way— young, dark, tall, taller than David, her feet sheathed in impossibly pointy and spiky-heeled boots or sandals, depending on the season. She waved at Marla now, from a table across the room.

What would an onlooker assume about their party of four? Marla often wondered. Marla and David could be the parents; Sloane their daughter; Griffin the grandfather. They embraced and exclaimed over cold cheeks, Sloane kissing Marla's hair and asking about her health, the men clasping hands. Griffin, seventy-three years old today, was still striking: half-Hawaiian and half-Swiss, his white hair thick, combed back from his broad brown forehead, his eyes a wild blue. David, who had taken to shaving his head, was Marla's age, fifty, "a real birthday," Griffin commented. "A birthday worth taking note of." Sloane, meanwhile, was a mere twenty-seven. David met her three years ago. They got married almost immediately, while Marla and Griffin lived together for a long time before going to the courthouse on a rainy spring afternoon for a brief but, to her, poignant civil ceremony. He gave her a bouquet of daisies and tulips, and a large solitaire diamond ring, which she loved more than she liked to admit.

Rosa's had once been a railroad house. Marla was one of the designers hired to assist with the renovations, which made her feel proprietary whenever she dined there. She loved the grittiness of the warehouse district, the dramatic entrance into the soaring space, the hand-blown chandeliers, the floor-to-ceiling slate fireplace. She liked remembering the way the building had looked the first time she saw it, filled with debris and dust, like a scene from a natural disaster or war zone. Before/after.

They settled in their usual places. Sloane was the one who took care of everyone, and she beckoned the waiter now. Marla ordered a glass of wine, Griffin a scotch, David his usual club soda with a splash of cranberry juice. Sloane said she'd start with a soda too—her office at the news station sucked the moisture out of everything, she was parched. Sloane had a funny crooked nose, and if she got it fixed her face would be perfect, and lose its character. She might get it fixed, Marla thought, when she got older, and missed being pretty.

"The worst thing about being sick is that I didn't buy anyone birthday presents," Marla told the husbands.

"That *is* the worst thing," David said.

"Though I for one am happy to accept late gifts," Griffin added. He was getting fidgety—he wanted his scotch. Marla stroked his arm.

"What did Sloane get you?"

"A fancy new digital camera. I'm using it for the book." David was working on illustrations for a children's book, an updated version of Icarus.

"And the Eric Clapton box set," Sloane said.

"Perfect." Marla smiled. She and David had seen Clapton in concert six times. They brought Josh along to one of those concerts when he was only five. David had torn filters off unsmoked cigarettes and given them to Josh to use as earplugs.

"Ah, here's our young man now," Griffin said. He looked as if he might rub his hands together, like a greedy fox in a fable.

Marla admired her Merlot. The color was jewel-like, and she swirled it against the sides of the glass, not for the legs but for the stained-glass, saturated red. Sitting among other people, the color in her hair touched up that afternoon, a few pounds lighter, she felt delicate and shiny, like something spun from fine filament. She took a sip of wine. Sloane and Griffin were discussing cures for insomnia, from which he suffered. Marla put on her reading glasses and examined the menu, though she always ordered the stuffed cannelloni.

The maître d' seated a young couple at the table next to theirs. The boy wore a denim jacket, which he slipped off and slung over his chair. On the arm of the jacket, right next to Marla, was an embroidered design. A globe, with turquoise seas and purple land. She inhaled sharply, coughed. She looked at the world again. The small black "x" and the fine cursive writing. *You are here.* She knew this jacket. She knew this black x. Her blood raced. She tried to catch David's eye, but he was in love with his lovely wife, and kept his eyes on her.

"You can't *try* to go to sleep," Sloane explained. "That's what this article I read says. Instead, you have to 'let go of waking.' Don't you love that?"

The tables at Rosa's were close together. Marla could, if she wanted to, put out her hand and touch the jean jacket. Why did this boy have Josh's coat? He appeared to be a few years younger than Josh was now, long-faced, with thick bangs over his eyes, pimples on his chin. No one she recognized. Josh hadn't worn the jacket for years, of course. She hadn't known when he gave it away, or lost it, or had it stolen. He was out of touch. She didn't understand it. She hated traveling—she blamed her childhood, all that moving around when she was growing up; her evangelical parents, wearing their poverty like a medal. *God will provide.* And in the meantime, they stayed one step ahead of the creditors. Marla left home when she was sixteen.

The waiter was back. He took their orders. Sloane went to the restroom, and Griffin stepped outside for a smoke; he allowed himself three cigarettes a day, though sometimes, Marla knew, it was more. Marla leaned toward David, breathing in his gingery scent. "Mine," she whispered—an old nickname she still used sometimes, so worn that it had lost its original meaning and was now just a sound that meant, hey. "Mine, look. The kid next to me. The jacket." At first David didn't understand. Then he did. The young man sensed their attention. "Is there a problem?" he asked. The waiter hadn't carded him. He was drinking a beer. His waif girlfriend sipped coke through a bendy straw.

"No problem." David smiled his easy smile. David, the former musician, the former pot head, the former hippie. Now he wore shirts from the Banana Republic. He ran five miles a day. His head was the hip kind of bald—he looked younger than when he'd had a ponytail. "My friend and I were just wondering. Where'd you get that jacket?"

The boy glanced at the coat, as if he couldn't remember what he had worn. "A guy gave it to me."

"It's my son's," Marla explained. "*Was* my son's."

"Just a weird coincidence," David said.

"Pretty weird," the boy nodded. He obviously didn't believe them.

"That globe, embroidered on the arm? Josh's high school girlfriend sewed that. He always wanted to travel." Marla looked at the girlfriend, hoping for some reaction.

"Awesome," she murmured, nibbling a breadstick.

"So, do you know Josh? Did you work at Figaro's, or the New World Bakery?" Marla's voice was louder than she intended.

"Marla," David said.

"I'm just wondering. If you saw him recently, within the last year say, or if he *gave* you the jacket, you know, a long time ago."

The boy looked at her through his bangs. "A long time ago." He turned back to his beer.

Marla's impulse was to grab the coat and run. What could "a long time ago" possibly mean to this kid? She looked at the coat, and gauged the distance between the table and the door. She imagined everything happening in slow motion.

"I just want to know where Josh is," Marla said to David. The boy shook his head, the girl giggled. Marla didn't care what that punk thought of her. She finished her wine in one large swallow.

Josh hadn't called, or written, or emailed, in four months. Weren't there internet cafes everywhere now? How hard could it be? And when, exactly, Marla wondered, should they contact the authorities? And who were the authorities, anyway? "He wants to get lost for a while," David always said. "He's just finding his way." These were Josh's words. *Don't worry about me, I just want to wander, untethered. I'll be in touch next summer.* That was what he wrote to them, back in November. A postcard from Turkey: a Thanksgiving joke, from the culinary institute dropout who was now intent on "getting lost."

Did summer mean June? August?

Marla and David had wanted more children. Marla wanted three or four. After Josh she had a miscarriage, and then a stillbirth, and then she was too sad to try again. Not just sad; she fell into a severe depression, rescued only by hospitalization and medication. The memory of that dark time—how quickly she had descended, how treacherous the climb out—still lurked, black and threatening.

By the time Josh was seven, adoption felt like less of an option. David was working fifteen-hour days, launching his graphic design business, while Marla worked as a bookkeeper for a couple of restaurants, a furniture store, a dry cleaners. On weekends David played bass in a bluegrass band. Marla was too old to act the part of the groupie, as she had done when they were first together. "You won't want me to play in a band when we're old," he told her then. She insisted she would never stand in the way of his true passions. Things looked different at thirty, thirty-two, thirty-three, but she kept her naïve promise. Those weekend nights, she lay in bed alone, waiting for the inevitable stumble on the stairs, the humming and whistling. He'd pass out next to her, his breath reeking. Once, he got up to go to the bathroom and peed in a potted plant.

When Josh was in third grade, Marla went back to school for her interior design degree. She got a job managing a store called The *LIVING* Room, which is where she met Griffin. He was in his late fifties, a professor of urban planning, long divorced, four grown children with whom he shared cordial conversation, as if they were former students—favorites, but students nonetheless. They ended up in places where he had taken them on sabbaticals or summer teaching gigs: one in Italy, one in Denmark, and two in England. His ex-wife lived in London to be closer to them. They called Griffin once a month or so; he didn't think about them much in between, though after the phone calls he was cheerful, as if he had accomplished something without trying, and the economy of effort pleased him.

After Marla and David divorced, she moved in with Griffin. David quit drinking. Josh divided his time between his two parents. Marla felt a queasy guilt, thinking back on Josh's adolescence. *Abdication* was the word that came to mind. She had abandoned the post of motherhood. Oh, she was there in body, just not in spirit. And Josh knew it.

Griffin returned to the table, then Sloane. Marla didn't say anything to either of them about the jacket, though she could feel it there, like a warm spot in an otherwise cold body of water. When the waiter arrived with plates of food, Griffin ordered a bottle of Merlot. Sloane, who relished her Chardonnay, who usually would have been on her second glass by now, asked for Pellegrino. At which point, Marla grasped the situation.

"Sloane," she said. "You're pregnant."

Sloane looked at David, who said, simply, "Yes."

"Wow, that's wonderful," Marla said. It was far from wonderful. In fact she had been dreading this moment for months. She reached across the table to grasp Sloane's hand. "Why didn't you say something, for heaven's sake?"

"We didn't want to take focus from the celebration," Sloane said. She beamed with obvious pleasure.

"This news trumps the birthday. Doesn't it, Griffin?"

Griffin agreed, and kissed Sloane's cheek. "You're in for a great adventure," he said. "Congratulations." He began eating his lasagna.

"Yes, by all means." Marla's voice sounded miserly, and she hated that. They all knew her too well, especially David. She lifted her glass but didn't wait for the others to do the same; just drank.

Sloane, liberated now to talk about what she really wanted to talk about, discussed their plans between bites of pumpkin ravioli. Her employer's maternity leave policy was more generous than most but not, as she said, "Scandinavian or anything." David would stay home and take care of the baby, since he worked at home anyway.

Marla was Sloane's age when she had Josh. David was pushing the rewind button, picking up where they had left off. No doubt David and Sloane would have not just this child but *children*, and Marla would be expected to remember the babies' birthdays with gifts and cards, she would have to hear detailed progress reports about turning over and sitting up and first words, she would have to go through it all and be a source of support. Would the babies call her Marla? Aunt Marla? *Grandma?* Meanwhile, Marla's finger was on the fast forward button. Tending to the needs of her old man would launch her prematurely into her own old age. Her old man—what they used to call their boyfriends. But Griffin *was* her old man. Twenty-three years older than she and David. And she and David were twenty-three years older than Sloane. And Josh was twenty-three.

Marla felt a bleak pleasure in doing the math.

"David is a wonderful father," Marla said. She could feel his eyes on her, his attempt to console her with a look, but she wasn't interested. *My friend and I were just wondering . . .* She put her arm out as if stretching, and grazed Josh's jacket with her fingertips. The boy didn't seem to notice.

"Have you forgotten the Sears episode?" David asked Marla.

"Everything turned out all right."

"I was so worn out in those days—broke, working all the time, drinking."

"We were poor," Marla agreed.

"One Saturday I went to Sears. They were having a sale on something, tools I needed, I don't remember. Marla was sick with flu, so I took Josh with me. He was three or four years old, wearing his Davy Crocket hat and the cowboy boots his grandparents gave him. I paid for the tools, went home, and about an hour later the phone rang. 'Do you have a little boy, coonskin hat?' I'd *forgotten* him."

"You didn't!" Sloane said.

"Kids survive," Griffin said. "They survive everything."

Except when they don't, Marla thought. "Remember the time Josh went to his friend's house by the reservoir, and brought home a shoebox full of bones?" She didn't know why she recalled that particular day. It had nothing to do with the Sears story, which was David's way of apologizing for the past. "He was so excited. He insisted he had discovered some prehistoric site, and found dinosaur bones. They were cat bones, weren't they, David?"

But David didn't remember that story. How Josh had tried to put the bones together, skull, spine, tail, how he wanted to keep the box in his closet but Marla made him throw it away. She scrubbed his hands with a nailbrush. That night, tucking him in, she found him touching his face. What are you doing? she asked. His fingers pressed along his brow, probed forehead, cheeks. *There are bones under here,* he said, amazed. He traced his jaw, his chin. *I'm a skeleton.*

Maybe Josh was dead. Maybe his passport had been stolen, so no one could identify him. He was lying in a morgue drawer, in Istanbul or Brussels, waiting for Marla. David, meanwhile, had armed himself, a replacement child at the ready.

"What was that kid's name?" David was asking. "That friend with the squirrel bones, or whatever they were?"

"Cat," Marla said. "At the time you said they were cat bones."

"Pablo, wasn't it? I remember that kid." This was David, drawing her back from the edge.

"His mother was from Costa Rica. She was hired as a nanny, by a widower with three kids. She ended up marrying her boss, even though he always called Pablo 'The Peasant.' 'Tell El Campesino it's time for dinner.'"

"How awful." Sloane shook her head.

Marla shrugged. "Things were different then."

"Absolutely true." Griffin smiled, a funny half smile. He'd had too much wine, Marla thought; while everyone was finishing dinner, he'd polished off the bottle.

David and Sloane debated the merits of roasted pears versus limoncello tiramisu. Sloane rested a palm against her flat belly, as if she could already feel the baby kicking. Marla rolled her eyes behind the dessert menu. "Do you want to split the chocolate sponge cake?" she asked Griffin. He looked blank. She nudged him with her foot. "Sponge cake? Griffin? Are you okay?"

"A little headache's all."

"I hope you're not getting my cold," she said. "I started out with headache too." She began reviewing her early symptoms, but now Sloane was alert, paying close attention to Griffin, and Marla stopped talking. Sloane came around to Griffin's seat and made him smile, repeat a sentence, lift his arms. He obeyed as if the exercises were routine postprandial behavior. Except he couldn't quite obey. The arms did not lift. The sentence trailed away. Everything happened fast, and slowly too; Sloane commanding David to call 911, then directing the restaurant staff to clear the nearby tables and make a path for the EMTs. The surrounding diners moved reluctantly toward the bar, carrying drinks and plates of food, wanting to keep their front row seats for the show—or that was how it felt to Marla. How could this be happening? Griffin insisted he was fine, but he seemed unable to see Marla or Sloane, and his speech was slushy. He complained of headache, said something about his shoes—he had to take them off or put them on—Marla couldn't make any sense of it. The panic was bracing, an open window in a closed-up room.

"It's okay, honey, help is coming, David has called an ambulance." Griffin looked at her with waning comprehension. His handsome face had gone slack and gray. She was afraid of him.

The EMTs arrived, two efficient, serious young men dressed in blue uniforms, like police officers. One man was black, one white. Marla tried to listen to Sloane's instructions but her head was buzzing. Was she having some kind of episode too? Could it be contagious? No. Just too much wine, mixed with regret, and a shot of adrenaline. What a cocktail, she thought. Next time she'd pass.

"Give me your car keys," Sloane was saying. "I'll take your

car. David will drive you in our car. We'll follow the ambulance to the hospital. Everything is going to be all right." Griffin lay on the gurney, his left hand curled and limp. Sloane relayed facts to the EMTs, the exact time she had noticed the onset of symptoms and the nature of those symptoms. Sloane, the consummate producer, as if Griffin's collapse were one of her television news segments.

Now it was time to leave. Marla, trembling, put on her cape, gathered coats from chairs. She made her way among the other tables with their votive candles and square porcelain salt and pepper shakers; she'd chosen those shakers, and the square white plates, and the glassware, and the silverware with its heavy, smooth, satisfying handles. She crossed the threshold back into the cold night, walked across the parking lot, again—hurrying now—only this time it was David's arm she leaned upon. The EMTs loaded Griffin like cargo into the back of the ambulance.

Marla got into David's car. He followed the ambulance. Sloane was still at the restaurant, settling their bill or something, Marla didn't know. Sloane, pregnant! Ten weeks along. Marla could hear herself weeping but couldn't connect the sounds to herself. What now, she kept thinking. What now? And: Shouldn't she have stayed with her husband, accompanied him in the ambulance? David said it was better to let the medical team do their work. "Griffin knows you're right behind him." But how could he know? He had been so confused. All that gibberish about his shoes. Marla shook her head. She was in shock, probably. David guided her through it. David was sober and clear-headed, and he was married now to someone who knew what to do in an emergency, not like Marla, who had ignored what was happening and prattled on about her own stupid cold.

Sloane's baby would be in her good, capable hands. She would do everything right. He would love her always.

David pulled into the hospital lot. He helped Marla out

of the car. She felt old, and weak. David seemed ten years younger than she, twenty; she was bent and stiff and aching, her joints sore, her muscles tired. She remembered getting dressed for the evening, applying mascara, wrapping the velvet scarf around her neck—it all seemed like a long time ago.

They approached the emergency room entrance. They had walked together through these hospital doors before—his mother's heart attack, Josh's broken leg, Marla's dark time. They knew the way. David took her hand, which was when she revealed what she'd been hiding in the folds of her cape: the denim jacket.

"Honey," David said. The globe on the sleeve shone and glittered, even after all this time. *You are here.*

"Mine," Marla said.

Mystery Date

At night Elena walks the dog and does not permit herself a glass of bourbon until she gets home. Everything now runs according to the schedule. People no doubt blame Elena, for mucking things up so completely. There's a gesture Elena makes when thoughts start going this way, her hand sweeping the air in front of her like a Buddhist with a fistful of straw, clearing the path of gnats.

The situation is almost funny when you think about it. Or it would be funny, if it were someone else's life you were talking about and not your own. She imagines that the people in this town, this Iowa town where she grew up, they've probably all had a good laugh, even as they act concerned when they see her in the grocery store, in the library, at the post office.

"Here's to one day at a time," Frank says every night, lifting his glass. Frank is her neighbor, and her best friend at the moment.

The days are long. Because of their length, the schedule is essential. The schedule is written in black marker and posted on a bulletin board that used to display invitations to birthday parties, Field Day ribbons, school pictures of other people's children, post cards, a typed-up and faded list of Phone Numbers in Case of Emergency. Now the state of emergency is perpetual. The numbers in case of emergency are on speed dial.

At least Elena has enough money to live on. Her parents left her some, and then there was an insurance settlement after a car accident a few years ago, money she miraculously invested at the right time and in the right dot com stock, getting out before the thing tanked. She is not wealthy, but she has plenty to live on, the house and car both paid off. And she takes occasional HR consulting jobs, clients she's known for years. She works from home—email, fax, FedEx.

From 9:00 to 10:00, Elena walks the dog. Frank stays with Maddie, Elena's daughter. He lives alone since the death of his partner—the person he spent twenty years calling his "roommate." He still says "roommate," out of habit perhaps, even to Elena, for whom no such euphemisms are necessary. Elena loves gay men and she especially loves Frank because he reads poetry to Maddie, the Brownings and Tennyson and sometimes Robert Lowell and Elizabeth Bishop who, Frank senses, is Maddie's favorite, though admittedly it's difficult to tell, since the night meds zone her out. Frank says that she rarely speaks but if he stops reading she sits up, waiting for him to continue. She once murmured, after Frank read Bishop's "The End of March," *a kite string, but no kite, a kite string, but no kite*, over and over, until Frank held her fidgeting hands and recited Whitman to quiet her.

Frank's lover did not die of AIDS (as people often assume). He was training for a marathon, running at 4:00 a.m., and some drunk guy, leaving his girlfriend's house after a fight, swerved off the road and hit him with his Ford pickup, in spite of the reflective vest and reflective shoes and reflective hat that Frank's lover was wearing. In spite of the fact that Frank's lover was running on the *sidewalk*.

Because of technicalities that do not bear thinking about, the drunk driver got off scot-free.

Maddie should maybe be hospitalized except that she threatened to do terrible things to herself if Elena put her back in the hospital—went into detail about the loopholes and the escape hatches and the things you can sharpen secretly and use on yourself—and so for now, no hospital. Elena isn't that brave. She just walks this careful tightrope and doesn't think about how there's no end in sight. Every two weeks she takes Maddie to her psychiatrist, who adjusts dosages, tries new combinations, Klonopin, Remeron, Effexor, and says, let's just wait and see how it goes. During the day, occupational therapy. It's all on the schedule: breakfast, *The Today Show*, the yoga DVD, watercolors or macramé, lunch, Eiffel Tower jigsaw puzzle, nap, dinner, television, bedtime, Frank.

Things have to change. That's what Frank says, in his cordial, tender way: Sweetie, things will change. A week, a month, a year. At some point, something else will happen. While Elena waits for the something else, she takes her walks, noting the streetlamp, the lilac tree on the corner almost in bloom, the buckled place in the sidewalk she reminds herself not to trip on. She looks inside the lit-up rooms, the men inside watching television, the women in the kitchen cleaning up or preparing lunches for the next day, the teenagers on their phones or computers. Tonight, the same as ever.

Except for this: Along with her cell phone, which she always carries in case Something Happens, Elena has brought her wallet. She can feel it in the pocket of her jacket, bumping against her hip with every step.

Inside the wallet, her debit card, credit cards, $300 cash.

For now, she is simply walking the dog. Florence belongs, or used to belong, to Elena's boyfriend Tony (*sweep, sweep*). Florence suffered a long period of mourning for her master, during which time Elena was coldhearted, told her straight up the things that Tony had neglected to explain before he left. Like, for example, he lied. He wasn't coming back to get her. As much as Elena suffered Tony's departure, as much pain and humiliation as she endured, she believes that Florence suffered more. A man leaving a woman is one thing, but a man who abandons his dog is, Elena believes, the worst kind of person of all.

Florence in any case has become neurotically attached to Elena. Florence is part cocker spaniel, part maybe whippet. She is a mess of a small skinny black dog with a too-long tail but beautiful insistent intelligent eyes that plead with Elena for attention. Florence has an unfortunate yappy bark, and she sometimes pees on herself with excitement. These are her main flaws. If Elena wanted a dog, which she doesn't, particularly, she would get a dog the size of a small horse. A Newfoundland, or English Mastiff. She would get a dog that would take up so much space you couldn't think about anything else as long as that dog was in the room.

But Florence couldn't help who she was or what had happened to her. "You're a good girl," Elena says.

The dog wags her absurd tail, her whole body curving into a horseshoe shape with the pleasure of being acknowledged, of being praised, of hearing at last the human voice of love.

Elena looks into the houses. There's the living room where she spilled red wine on the new carpeting, the guest room where she had furtive conversations with someone else's husband, the kitchen where she lit birthday-cake candles for a friend bald from chemo. Some of her childhood friends' parents still live where they lived when Elena went over to play. She remembers the Mystery Date board game at Debbie Haymaker's house, a game her own mother, flush with second-wave feminism, railed against. The board had a white plastic door in its center. Eventually—Elena couldn't remember exactly how it worked, though she could still remember the commercial's jingle—you opened the door to find out who your date was. The game taught girls, correctly Elena thought, that life was about waiting. Debbie always wanted the Dream Date, clean cut in his white suit. He was the guy you were supposed to want. Getting the Dream Date meant that you won the game. But even then, at eight years old, Elena was more intrigued by the Dud—the wrong-side-of-the-tracks boy, scruffy, unshaven, shifty, hot.

Frank says he liked the skier.

She remembers also kissing Thomas Kerby behind the Kerbys' garage, the stack of firewood pressing into her back and leaving an unraveled spot in her sweater. She remembers the Schultzes' parakeets escaping from their cage, Barbara Kramer falling off her bike and breaking her wrist, bone poking through skin, and the pair of old women, sisters, who tended the flowers at their own headstones (those end dates left eerily blank). Florence has learned the routine, which houses create interest, where she can pee while Elena pauses to place a mental checkmark in each box.

The Corrells, Hansons, Mitchells, Schultzes, Whites.

Pauses but does not stop because she won't be one of those creepy single women who wander the streets at night looking into people's windows. Are there creepy single women who do that? She's not sure, she's never seen them, but she senses she could easily become a type, if she isn't one already: small town strumpet, laughingstock, pathetic hanger on. Mother of suicidal girl.

Sweep. Sweep. Sweep.

And her old house. She stops there now. If life were a movie, a phantom image of her mother waving on the front porch would appear. But there is no such image and no such mother. Did her mother ever wave to her from the front porch? That image belongs to some generic childhood, not Elena's, not even in Iowa. The living room is painted red, because red is a fashionable color to paint walls now, whereas when she was growing up in that house the walls were covered in fake brown paneling. She will always feel that she has more rights to the house than the people who now live in it, and the red walls, though pretty, are all wrong.

Back up the hill, past the cemetery where her mother is buried, and those two old sisters, too. Mom doesn't wave at Elena from this place either, there's just the darkness, the trees, the stone wall that lines the cemetery—the boneyard, Maddie calls it—just her mother there, dead. *Hey, Mom*, she always says, and Florence perks up, yaps, pees.

Then back home.

9:57.

Elena stands on the sidewalk in front of her house. Green shutters that need sanding and painting, Christmas lights still strung in the tree in the yard though Christmas has long since passed, brown leaves on the porch. What would someone else see, someone who didn't know the story, didn't know about the ruined marriage, how Elena left the good husband, a high school biology teacher and track coach, *a nice guy*, for the bad-boy lover? The Dud. But everyone does know. Knows how she was punished for her mistake, how her son chose to live with his father—the son who barely speaks to her now—while the daughter stayed with her, except for the times the daughter was in the hospital, and except for the time she ran away, hitchhiked to New Orleans.

Then—and here's the best part—then the lover, *ha ha*, after all that, the lover left her. *After all that*. Left Elena and Florence, too.

Dear Frank. If, tonight, Elena took her walk and kept going and did not come back, Frank would take care of Maddie. He would call Maddie's father, who now lives in Santa Fe. And the father, and Elena's son, would welcome Maddie home. And the stepmother too, no doubt—because of course Elena's husband remarried, successfully. Of course he is not the one who ended up alone.

9:58.

A cab to the Greyhound station in Des Moines, a bus departing at 11:15, arrival in Chicago at 6:00 a.m. She'd pay the cabbie double to take Florence home. No pets allowed on the bus—she's read the rules. She's read them to Florence too, and convinced herself that Florence would be okay.

She stands on the porch steps. Inside, Frank turns on the TV. He has her drink ready. She can see it, on the coffee table, resting on one of the coasters Maddie wove all those years ago, in summer camp. He has prepared her a plate of grapes and cheese. They will watch a *Law and Order* rerun. Every night, 10:00 is the edge of the cliff, and Elena gratefully steps off it. Frank steps off with her. They hold hands, close their eyes, and fall, grateful for the rush of air, not thinking about the crash landing. There's his martini, and so polite is Frank that he waits for her before he takes even one sip. He's courtly, formal, until he's had his cocktail, then he becomes damp-eyed, and his ruddy face takes on a sheen that Elena thinks of as Vodka Shimmer, as if it's a shade of Almay blush. Two drinks and he has to blot his eyes with a handkerchief he keeps folded in a neat rectangle in his pocket, as if he's somebody's grandfather. Three, and he calls her the next day, apologizing.

9:59.

Maddie's room is dark. Her sleep is so deep, Elena often hovers in the doorway and listens for the sounds of breathing, the way she did when her children were babies. All of Maddie's medications are under lock and key, a small metal box that Elena keeps in her closet, on the top shelf, as if the situation were simply a matter of keeping certain things out of Maddie's *reach*.

How desperate is the woman who walks away and keeps walking? People would shake their heads in wonder. People would say, I knew it, Ever since, Can you imagine, Of course she always, Life's not easy, But you have to, You can't, On the other hand, What are you going to do, At least, Anyway, That's the way it goes, She always was a troubled child.

Elena steps onto the front porch, pats her pocket as if it held a talismanic stone.

Open the door for your . . . Mystery Date!

She does open it. She walks into the house, the house she bought with her husband all those years ago when they moved back to Iowa to raise their family. Of course she does. She isn't going anywhere. She wouldn't, ever. Momentary madness! Caretaker burnout! It was just a fleeting something or other.

And the living room clock chimes 10:00. And she shuts and locks the door. And she unhooks Florence's leash from her collar. And she hangs the leash on its hook.

She puts her wallet back inside her bag. Zips it up. *Sweep.*

Florence dances on her hind legs like a circus animal, ready for her treat. The trick embarrasses her, but she can't help it. This is all I know to do for you, her smart eyes say. Sorry, but this is all I've got.

The opening dialogue of the *Law and Order* episode murmurs from the living room. "We've seen this one before," Frank calls. But it doesn't matter. They'll watch anyway. They never remember who the culprit is until the very last minute.

Bodies

Beth puts a finger over the large freckle, oddly shaped, that has always sat just below her left knee, always, so it's a birthmark maybe, something they can use to identify her body if they ever need to, like the tiny scar below her ear. She is obsessed with this idea lately, identifying bodies, something she heard on television or else from her older brother, or someone talking. Another Beth Reynolds, a new girl, has started at Beth's school, one grade ahead of her, and already there have been mix-ups with library books and phone calls and recess games. Beth worries. If she died and her name was in the newspaper, nobody would know which Beth it was. We'd use your middle name, her mother says, and Beth nods, says *Elizabeth Lockwood Reynolds* over and over until it doesn't sound like her name anymore. Her freckle is her freckle though. She can put one finger over the brown dot below her knee and press and nothing changes. She is otherwise freckleless, she is otherwise eight years old and she sticks her legs straight out in front of her on the flat stone steps in between the warmed marigold flowerbeds, the sharp peaty smell drifting up to her as she eats a piece of white bread with peanut butter on it. She made the snack herself. She likes making her own snacks and anyway her mother is busy with the neighbor. The neighbor stopped by on her way home. The two women are inside drinking coffee, sitting on the pink couch, while the neighbor's little boy goes in and out of the house so often they do not need to think about him until it is time to leave.

Beth saw it on TV: how they spread the peanut butter on the white bread and it looked so good, so smooth and deep like thick frosting, so she makes a snack like this only without the jelly it is like eating paste. She skips past the pool to the lilac tree, setting the rest of the bread with the peanut butter on a branch. The birds will eat it. Birds like bread and they like peanut butter so they will eat it. Maybe a cardinal will come— Beth has just learned about the state bird and the state bird of Illinois is a cardinal. Her favorite state thing is the white-tailed deer and her second favorite is the violet and her least favorite is the blue gill. It is May, she loves school, she loves her mother, she lives in a house, she sees the marigolds' sunny heads, yellow and orange, the grass is thick and new, the sky is high and blue, she skips into the house, kittens born in her mother's closet, five kittens but one died, the mother sat on it, the mother smothered it at birth probably because there was something wrong with it, that's what they told Beth, that's what Beth knows, and she checks to see if their eyes have opened yet, no they have not, look at the mama cat's nipples poking out so rudely like the dog's pink thing, look at her dark yellow furry belly with those wet pink fingers sticking out, then in her room and out of her room and the mothers talking and laughing in their polite voices downstairs, talking and talking, and then calling, calling the boy, time to go, where are you, it is time, and calling and calling.

Beth's mother and the neighbor are not even very good friends. The neighbor was just driving by. She has just come from Beth's school where she registered her boy for kindergarten for the fall. The neighbor wore a spring suit for the occasion, light green with tiny flowers on it, a skirt and blazer, a white blouse. The boy wore a sailor suit and new red Keds. The mothers drank coffee and the boy ran in and out of the house, showing them the things he had found: a stone, a feather, a leaf, a ladybug.

Now Beth runs outside with the mothers and they yell the little boy's name. His name is Christopher. It's fun calling him and the mothers' rising voices are exciting and different; it is a game, and also serious, and Beth runs with racing heart to all the places or almost all the places he might be—the front steps, under the willow, in his mother's car, in the garage. Perhaps he is hiding from them, and Beth will be the one to find him. Then the neighbor and her son can go home and Beth can have her mother all to herself again.

From the patio Beth sees her brother walking toward the house with his friend Louis, carrying something. She yells to her mother, here comes Greg, he's got something. They think for a second, Beth and the mothers, that maybe he is carrying Christopher, that maybe that is the answer, even though it makes no sense, even though if he were carrying the boy in that position it would mean the boy was hurt, and Greg would be walking faster or running or behaving in some other alarmed way and he is not. They yell to him, Greg, Greg, have you seen Christopher? He is confused, No, but he runs over to them now, he hears what is in their voices. He is carrying a sleeping bag that he left at his friend's house, a green sleeping bag with a red flannel lining.

Then it occurs to them, finally, where they must look.

He is at the bottom. He is in the deep end.

It is a spot that Beth will never forget, that one spot in the deep end. He was maybe playing with a net that is floating in the water, he dropped the net and was trying to get it. People talked about this later, what must have happened, why he was near the pool, they had told him, they had warned him, also he knew how to swim, also he had been such a good swimmer last summer at the lake, also he swam even better than his older sister, also he had been a little fish last summer, also he was just in the house he was just here, also.

The mothers see him there, at the bottom. The mothers scream. Beth's mother cries, Greg, get him, see if you can get him. Greg jumps in with all his clothes on. He tries swimming to the bottom of the deep end. He comes up once and goes down again. He is twelve. He is a good swimmer but he is twelve and when he gets to the bottom he does not have enough air to lift the boy and carry him to the surface. He tries. The boy is at the bottom. Greg comes up again. I can't get him, Greg says. I can't get him. He swims to the side. He climbs out of the pool. It is a bright day, the sun shining on Greg's wet brown hair. The cement around the pool underneath Beth's bare feet is warm. The neighbor takes off her black pumps, jumps in, in her green suit. She goes right to the bottom. She swims right down there and she grabs her boy and brings him up and swims to the side and Beth's mother takes him. She lays him on the cement. How long has he been there? Greg and Louis and Beth stand by the pool but not too close to the mothers, no, on the other side of where the mothers are. Beth's mother puts her mouth on Christopher's mouth. She blows into it. In between breaths she makes terrible sounds. She does not tell Beth to go play now, does not tell Greg and Louis to take Beth inside, turn on the TV, something.

That's what he ate for lunch, the neighbor cries, the water and soggy bread crusts gushing from the boy's mouth and the boy does not look like the boy, eyes closed, face tight, hair plastered down, clothes plastered down, wet skin shining, limbs spread, vomit and water. Call the ambulance, Beth's mother says, go in the house and call the ambulance, and the neighbor in her wet green suit and her stockings and her wet hair runs into the house and calls.

The boy just lies there.

The neighbor comes back outside. I don't think I gave them the address—I told them the street but I don't know the number. Beth's mother sends Beth and Greg to the front yard. Go wait for the ambulance, tell them where we are, wait on the front steps.

Louis runs home. Greg and Beth wait. They walk up and down the stone path. It'll be okay, don't you think it'll be okay, they'll fix him at the hospital, they have machines also in the ambulance when the ambulance comes the men will put him on a stretcher and they have machines inside the ambulance that can make him better. They have oxygen and shots they can give him. Greg tells Beth these things, explains to her how it will go. On the front steps of their house they wait, Greg's arms and legs goosefleshy in the breeze, wet threads from his cut offs clinging white against his leg, the oak trees making spotty shadows on his dark T-shirt. White oak is the state tree, Beth thinks, but she isn't sure if the oak trees in their yard are white oaks or some other kind. Beth is glad to stand with her brother who usually doesn't come out here with her on the front steps where she likes to watch cars go by or kids on bikes. She thinks of Christopher's house just down the street, a big yellow house with lots of yard and woods all around and a barn and even two horses. That house is empty right now because Christopher's sister is playing at a friend's house, and the father is at work, and everyone else from that family is here, in Beth's backyard.

It takes a long time for the ambulance to come. It feels like a very long time. Beth wonders what her mother is doing now. She wonders if Christopher is still throwing up or if he has stopped.

Then the ambulance. Beth and Greg jump up and down and wave at it as if they are on a deserted island and this is the ship that has finally sailed into view. They run ahead to the backyard to show the men where to go. The men are carrying bags and run clumsily. Greg and Beth wait on the patio. Everything takes a long time. Beth thought they'd just take him right away. The mothers maybe could have gotten him to the hospital by now. If they'd put him in the car. But the hospital is a ways away. Twenty minutes, maybe. Beth has seen it, a big brick building on a hill. They wait. After a long time the mothers run across the grass. Their faces.

Greg, take Beth to Louis's, Beth's mother says.

The mothers ride with Christopher to the hospital. Greg and Beth walk to Louis's house. Louis's mother has a gold tooth and brown worried eyes and wears a blue housecoat and speaks in a strong accent, not like other mothers. Louis's bald father wears a dark green uniform like the gas station man, his name sewn over one pocket in red cursive. Beth watches *Superman* on the black and white TV. Louis's mother keeps adjusting the antennae. She brings Beth food, peanut butter and marshmallow fluff sandwiches, something her mother never makes. The house smells of cooking. The house feels small. Beth has never been here before.

Greg disappears with Louis. She doesn't know where they go or what she's supposed to do. She eats half of the sandwich but it makes her feel sick. Louis's mother wrings her hands and frets and keeps looking out the window. Beth doesn't want to be rude, but she cannot eat that sandwich.

That night Beth's father comes home. He doesn't always come home. He stays in the apartment they have rented in Chicago. Her mother sometimes takes her to the Field Museum or the Art Institute which is her favorite because of the Thorne Miniature Rooms. On the nights her father doesn't come home, Beth's mother talks to him on the phone. Dinner plates are covered in foil and kept warm in the oven and then eventually after the phone call, moved into the refrigerator. The plates are white with little blue swirls around the edges like commas. Sometimes the food is thrown away and the plate is washed and dried and put back in the cabinet. This night, he comes home.

Beth does not sleep in her bed on this night. She sleeps on the pink couch. The couch where the mothers were sitting. She sleeps here with the afghan covering her. The parents are talking. They think she is already asleep but she isn't. She can hear the ice in her father's glass. The room is dark. Her mother is sitting in the wing chair by the window. Her father is sitting in the tub chair across the room. He is smoking a Pall Mall from the red pack and drinking scotch from his glass. Beth can peek at them because they think she is asleep and anyway they are not thinking about her right now. Her mother is weeping.

I'll never forget seeing his little head, she cries. I thought it was a football.

Her father's eyes are rimmed with red and he drops his head back, looks at the ceiling. All this is happening but Beth is on the couch and her mother and father are there so maybe it is okay after all. No one has said what happened, after the ambulance. No one has said what happened in the hospital.

The conversation is a soft murmur now, a few words, then quiet, then a few more words, like intermittent rain, a drop here and there, and soon Beth goes to sleep. That is the last night she hears any adults talk about it. They can't talk about it. The grown-ups can't. They don't know how to talk about it or else they talk about it when Beth isn't there or else they have sworn to each other never to say anything about it again.

Beth calls her best friend the next day, when it is clear what must have happened. Pray to God, her friend says now. If you pray hard enough, God will bring Christopher back. You just have to pray really hard. You just have to believe and it will happen. Neither Beth nor her friend have ever actually gone to church or been schooled in the ways of faith, but now her friend is fervent and sure. Beth listens to her voice on the other end. She presses the phone to her ear. She imagines her friend sitting cross-legged on her couch. She agrees that she will pray, but she does not after all.

At school, in line waiting for the bus, Denise Grassio whom everyone calls Denise Grassy Ass, tells Beth what Christopher's sister has been saying all day.

For a moment Beth can't breathe. She looks straight ahead, the cinder block walls, Gordon Jensen's ugly square head, someone's Flintstones lunchbox. Her whole body goes hot and tingly, like when they make you put your coat on in the winter ten minutes before the bus is even supposed to come and you have to stand in the hot corridor waiting, hat and mittens and scarves and you wish you could just go outside and wait in the cold. Why would Christopher's sister make up such a thing? Why would she tell people this lie? She sees herself on that day. How she checked the kittens, how she walked outside with the bread and peanut butter for the cardinals, the smell of lilac, the bright sky. How she put the bread in the tree and climbed down from the stone wall and went inside. Then the mothers couldn't find him. Then she helped them look for him. Then they found him. But Christopher's sister is saying, she has been telling everyone in the entire school—

She says you pushed him in.

Denise is still looking at her. Beth finally shakes her head. I did not, she says, as if she is fighting with Greg about some little thing, a lost G.I. Joe or the last slice of cake. The buses come. They line up, the usual row of caterpillars. The numbers are called. Beth's number is eleven. Number eleven is called and her line inches forward. Denise is in a different line and her line doesn't move. Mrs. Flynn, the bus driver, sits in her seat, her sleeves pushed up her big arms. Last year Mrs. Flynn gave Beth a rhinestone pin in the shape of a ballerina that Beth keeps in her jewelry box. Beth climbs the bus steps, legs tired.

Hey sweetie, Mrs. Flynn says. How's your day been?

Okay, Beth says. She takes the first seat, right behind Mrs. Flynn, so that Mrs. Flynn can keep an eye on her.

Outside: parking lot, grass, trees, cloud, sky, sky.

I've Looked Everywhere

I lost my cell phone yesterday. This afternoon I heard it ringing faintly from deep inside its hiding place: a totebag, purse, kitchen drawer, pocket? I tried tracking the sound—first it seemed to be coming from the bedroom, then the study—but just as I thought I was getting close, the battery must have lost power, or else the person hung up. I went through the possibilities. Not very many people have the cell phone number. You, my sister, my ex-husband, my massage therapist, my housepainter who is also, maybe, my boyfriend, though maybe not. I called them all, all except you and the ex-husband because he'd only call in case of an emergency and he'd try the landline first for that; and the housepainter, because I've called twice this week, and I don't want to appear desperate.

I decided to go to the library, to return the overdue books, but remembered that they are lost too. Three of them, checked out two months ago, and the fines have almost exceeded the value of the books. One was a book of poetry that I used to keep by my bed, because after you left I discovered that reading poetry before I went to sleep produced interesting, poetic dreams. The other was a biography of a child actor; I love stories about people doing drugs. And the third I can't remember.

I'm losing confidence, but not weight. I'm losing my glasses, my mind, my sense of balance. In yoga class I used to be able to do the tree pose and now I can't. I topple over like a badly constructed block tower. Everyone pretends not to notice because they're practicing their serene yoga faces. I'm losing estrogen, instant recall, the ability to spell words I have always known how to spell. The stocks I own are losing money, have lost money, are worthless. The country I live in is losing wars—against drugs, fat, violence, stupidity, invisible forces we can't name, enemies we've only imagined who now rightly despise us. I'm losing faith. Altitude. Ground. I've lost two husbands—one to heart failure, and one to a twenty-year-old—and children—one to her dreaded Peer Group, and the other to a cultish mentality about a particular heavy metal band that shall go unnamed. I lost my name, twice, and now I can't get it back again. I'm losing elasticity, skin and otherwise. Losing perspective. Losing my appetite, but not for food. I've lost the receipt to the beige dress I bought for my daughter's high school graduation that she said made me look like a matronly cow so I decided to wear the purple rayon pantsuit instead. Without the receipt, I'm stuck with the cowsuit, which hangs in my closet with many other articles of clothing my daughter has forbidden me to wear. I've lost my taste for older men because really, how much older can I go? I've lost my yen. For transatlantic travel, for driving a stick shift, for falling snow, loud dinner parties, loud noise of any kind except certain rock bands from an entirely different era, late-night phone calls. I've lost the lyrics to that song that is nevertheless stuck in my head: *Baby please don't go*, something something something . . . I've lost the left shoe from my favorite pair, the black sandals for whom I get regular pedicures in the summer, the sandals that I bought three years ago in Italy—you were with me. Do you remember the sandals? Where in God's name does a single black leather Milanese sandal go? Is it at your house? Under the bed, perhaps, or in your closet, with your shoes?

Old friends. The desire to be first in line. The desire to go at all. The need to fit in, to do what I'm told, to accept second best, to fight the good fight, to be quiet. I've lost the remote control—forever this time, my car keys, a pair of $200 sunglasses I promised myself I would never lose, three skin cancers off my back, the directions to your sister's summer house, the children's baby teeth, many important documents that I'm certain I had signed by a notary public but did not, apparently, store in a safe place, a charcoal sketch of my childhood home, and the Maxime Le Forestier album I bought in Quebec in 1975. On the list of lost things also is the list of things I keep meaning to do, and the list of things I'm sorry I did, though when I wake up at four in the morning, there they all are, crowded around my bedside like eager dogs, pawing my hand, begging me to scratch their ears.

I've lost my place in the book I'm reading, the negative for the picture of us I wanted to enlarge (standing on the stone steps, Lake Champlain behind us), the phone number for the acupuncturist my neighbor recommended. Both parents and a brother, six dogs, eight cats, four hamsters, three birds, and, I'm not kidding, a pear tree, which died of blight. The instructions to the Cuisinart, the breadmaker I got for my second wedding—and you tell me where a breadmaker could possibly be hiding. The extension cord I swear I bought last week, this week's *TV Guide*, my favorite pen.

I've looked everywhere.

Every day there's something else, things dropping away like the careless removal of clothing or make-up after a party, like the diamond earring that slips from my fingers into the bathroom sink and down the drain, disappearing so quickly it seems to have planned its daring escape. We both watch it fall, incredulous, as if this kind of thing never happens. You kindly take apart the pipes underneath the sink (still wearing your handsome evening clothes, crisp white sleeves rolled up to your elbows) but the earring is gone. You straighten, unroll your sleeves, pluck the remaining earring from my palm and drop it into the drain just like that, without looking at me. And I can't read the gesture, or the expression on your face; can't decide if what you mean is, See, it doesn't matter, it's just a *thing*; or, Now the two earrings will be together forever; or, Through your terrible carelessness, your inability to watch what you're doing, your consistently wretched sense of timing, you've sealed your fate, and mine.

There! Did you hear that? The phone—it's ringing again. Three rings, four. Now is the moment when I realize I could have just dialed the cell number myself, and tracked down the phone. "Dur," my oldest daughter would say. I stand in the middle of the room, six, seven, the afternoon light fading now, the shadows lengthening across the woven rugs. The rings stop. It must be later than I think, the way the light falls across the floors. The day must have gotten away from me, as it does sometimes. Does that ever happen to you? The day slipping by? Who knows where it goes. But it's late, in any case, it's starting to get dark, it's getting dark a lot earlier now, and in the mornings when I go for my walk, there's a chill, a dampness. Sometimes I wear a sweatshirt, my favorite one, faded blue, extra large, soft from many washings. The one you must assume, by now, that you've lost.

You Again

The poet pleads for a sign—she wants her dead to come back—and Corinne, on a folding chair in between Self-Help and Sports, accidentally says out loud what she is thinking: "But they never send a sign, do they?"

It's a Saturday in early June, and the poet reads to a dozen women who have come to hear her express their collective woes. Succor for the suckers, Corinne thinks. The bookstore's space for readings is cramped, the ceiling low. Corinne's voice is soft but audible—the tone she uses when she talks to herself at home, a running commentary that she realizes now is a bad habit, leading, as it does, to moments like these, when the lines between speaking and thinking blur. Her question is greeted at first with predictable surprise, but the group is intimate in their musty corner, wearing their northwestern uniform, Bjorns or Keens, lightweight fleece vests against the chilly morning, scarves wrapped skillfully around crepey necks. They don't act as scandalized as Corinne would've expected. They turn back to the poet as if for an answer.

The poet's gray spiky hair somehow goes spikier, like vibrating wires. She tilts her head, smiles at Corinne. "Not so far," she admits. "But I still listen." She emphasizes ever so slightly that last word, signaling that listening now would be an excellent idea for Corinne. She bites the inside of her lower lip to keep the words where they belong. The woman seated to her right edges her seat the tiniest bit further to the right in an *I've never seen this person before* gesture. She must be a disciple of Pilates; her posture is admirable. Her nails are manicured, the backs of her hands smoother than Corinne's, though Corinne is forty-six and this person must be approaching sixty. Estrogen, probably. She's found a supplier of patches or gels, a dealer she can count on. One hand clasps the other loosely in her lap. She wears a white skirt with small red polka dots, a departure from everyone else's dark and neutral colors. The woman senses Corinne's attention, and if she moves any further away from Corinne, she will tumble to the floor. Or she would, if she weren't wedged between Corinne and the hippie-grandma, whose purring, meaningful "mmms" punctuate the end of every poem.

The poet's life is not easy, that's for sure. A husband with Parkinson's, a father with Alzheimer's, an estranged brother—and then a shift to quantum gravity and elementary particles, which Corinne doesn't understand or care about—why do poets always want to write about physics? And then a series of garden poems that dote on irises. Go back to death, Corinne wants to say. That's what we came for.

Later Corinne will walk to the farmer's market for fresh flowers (okay, irises) and berries and honey and daikon radishes. She shifts in her chair, feels her *sit bones* as her yoga teacher says. She wishes she could check her phone. She has been successful up to this moment in not thinking about the phone, but once the thought leaps up, her hand opens and closes, itchy for phone-contact. He hasn't texted her, she knows. She knows he hasn't. She is a teenager again, waiting for a boy to call! Pathetic. Over and over, the same things. That's what the daikon radishes are for. She will try a new vegetable, at least. Last week it was some bitter greens whose name she can't remember now.

Anomia: the inability to recall names of people and objects. *Anomie:* Personal unrest that comes from a lack of purpose or ideals. Corinne can never remember which is which, so she has memorized the definitions.

After the polite applause, Corinne considers apologizing to the poet, making excuses—her medication, brain fog, clouding of consciousness, medication (did she say that already)?—but she decides not to. The other women are getting books signed. Corinne doesn't feel bad enough to buy a book. An apology without dropping the $15.95 wouldn't seem like much, to the poet. Who is, Corinne sees now, spiky-haired *and* tattooed. Some Celtic design, rings inside of rings, on her ankle. When she stands up, her drawstring pants reveal a dispiriting thong outline. All this effort, Corinne thinks. The yoga and tattoos and manicures and—thongs.

Outside, the day warming up, the day lovely, she pulls her phone from her bag. No new messages, no new emails, no new texts, no news from the man she loves and pines for and yes desires, *God* she wants him. Unseemly, how much. Focus, she thinks, gritting her teeth to prevent words from spilling out of her mouth. Maybe the habit started when she was a young mother, pushing the grocery cart through the store and murmuring to the baby. "Seven grams of sugar…That seems like a lot for spaghetti sauce, don't you think?"

Corinne and Gary, the father of her child, were together only three tiny years. Their marriage takes up almost no room in their respective stories. The divorce was amicable, or that's how they like to remember it. He was—is—gay. She visits him and his partner at their beach house. Very modern Thanksgivings, with the shared grown daughter and her boyfriend, and the interesting people Gary and Bruce have collected over the last two decades, and conviviality all around, aided by a lot of excellent wine over which much fuss is made. Sometimes, after three or four drinks, Bruce gets weepy, but everyone ignores him, as if he's a hypochondriac, or brain damaged. Corinne squeezes his arm, kisses his bald head. *Everything's okay, dear Bruce,* and he presses her hand damply to his cheek.

No, she won't call. She won't text.

At the market she sees Dr. Mosier selecting heirloom tomatoes. She gives him a wide berth. The town is too small, that's the truth! She does miss L.A. sometimes. "I am *depressingly* underfucked," she said at her last session, making Dr. Mosier smile. She likes making him smile. Once, she made him weep, and that seemed like a bad sign—making your therapist so sad for you that he cried. She buys the produce and a ribbon-tied bunch of perfect Japanese irises, and puts everything into the eco-friendly bag she keeps in her purse.

"I'm upping your dosage," Dr. Mosier had told her this week. "You may notice an increase in the symptoms, but they should abate after a few days. You just need to recalibrate." Ah. So she had, apparently, *calibrated* (calibrate: a comparison between measurements . . . one of known correctness, and the other . . . not so much?) and now, she is doing it again. The pills create a small space between one thing and the next, especially here, in the sunshine, in the rich June air, a pulsating moment right before the next one, and then again . . . right after. The sensation is not altogether unpleasant.

The other night she dreamed she was smoking pot for the first time in decades. She woke up feeling high.

He isn't going to call.

She drifts through the market, carried along by the buzz of people greeting each other, sunglasses and hats and dogs on leashes, groovy children in strollers holding pinwheels and waving as if they're in a parade. Under white canopies, vendors peddle organic goat cheese, handmade soaps, cinnamon rolls, exotic lettuces, free-range chickens, flats of bright annuals. A graying man in tie-dye plays guitar and sings (Gordon Lightfoot? really?); young people with clipboards and petitions stand in the middle of the closed-off street, accosting passersby with their white smiles and zeal, green this, green that. Corinne nods vaguely, she smiles at people she recognizes, she shares a brief exchange with a woman whose daughter used to be best friends with hers, she fawns dutifully over a colleague's baby. Two old homeless men argue laconically on a bench. "You just have to face it," one says to the other. "The days of a lot of money are over." Corinne wonders at this. When were those days? How much is a lot of money? She buys two enormous blueberry muffins and delivers them to the men, who nod their thanks, as if she's the waitress bringing their order.

A girl, maybe fifteen years old, stands in front of a massage booth playing violin. She looks like Corinne's sister: wispy figure, tilt of the head. A flash of memory, the two of them, jumping on hotel room beds . . . a weekend in San Diego with their father . . . *Keep it light, drink Fresca* . . . a commercial they loved, how the woman rose and fell in tantalizing slow motion, floating both up and down, while Corinne and Olivia, no matter how hard they tried, couldn't achieve such enviable airiness . . . *Fresca is the light diet soft drink.*

Oh, Olivia.

The smell of fresh basil, the smell of mint, of lavender, Corinne walks through the market, hums the ancient jingle, *Keep it light*—and there's the poetry reading lady, coming right toward her. They are taking the same route today, crossing the same items off their lists. They should have coffee, or a drink. Compare notes. Maybe she has a boyfriend, too. In her basket she carries Gerber daisies, stems girded with plastic tubes to keep them from bowing their heavy heads; beet and carrot greens spill rustically over the edge of the straw weave. The polka-dot skirt is girlish and summery in the bright day.

Corinne smiles and nods as they pass each other. She can't tell if the woman doesn't recognize her, or recognizes her all too well.

One martini. The cool bar, the dark bar, the bar almost empty (two o'clock in the afternoon) except for two boys—well, young men. Corinne sits three stools down from them, gives the bartender her order. Dry martini, very very dry, extra olives please, yes it's beautiful outside, a beautiful day. Mmm, perfect, thanks so much. She puts her cell phone by her elbow.

The man who doesn't call and doesn't text has a cell phone that he uses just for her—their private line. Perhaps his wife has discovered it. She has hurled it across the room, and the phone has clattered against the Tuscan tile of their kitchen, the phone now in plastic pieces, undial-able, uncall-able. Corinne always thinks (when she doesn't hear from him) that the worst has happened, that the world behind that red front door with the leaded stained glass is falling apart, because of Corinne. But disclosure is never the reason for his neglect. It's always something dreary and domestic, a forgotten dinner party, errant stepchildren, a broken garbage disposal.

Corinne knows the wife, though not well. She has spoken to her at a few functions. The wife works downtown in the building next to Corinne's. She's an optometrist, well-liked by her patients. He is not going to leave her. Corinne doesn't even want him to.

"Nostalgia is a trope of Japanese cinema," one of the boys says. His companion nods, they talk of Kurosawa, they talk of compressed space and carefully constructed scenes and dissolves and Corinne sips her drink, one drink, just one, alcohol a *contraindication*. Her brain is hard at work. Nerve cells, voltage-dependent sodium channels, electric signals straightening themselves out. *One in four women takes prescription drugs for mental health issues*, a morning headline announced. She lifts her glass in a toast to her neurons, so busy up there in her head. "The idea is to balance out the chemicals," Dr.

M. says. Good luck, she thinks. Or maybe she speaks it; there's a lull in the pretentious conversation.

"That must hurt," she says. The boys (they can't be more than twenty-two, easy in their bodies, seemingly unmarred by life, though she remembers well the particular suffering of the young heart) turn toward her. They've had a few beers. They smile. Carefree boys on a Saturday afternoon. She points to her own earlobes, then theirs. Plugs made of wood or bone, large flat buttons, are embedded inside stretched earlobe-flesh that Corinne wants to tell them will never ever be the same again. Don't they know that? Don't they get it?

"The gauges?" The dark-haired boy is the handsomer of the two. The other one, blond, wears a watchman's knit cap. He probably wears it all year long, no matter the temperature outside. That's the kind of hat it is. That's the kind of boy he is. She licks her lips. Just three or four sips left.

"It's a pretty gradual process," the knit cap says.

Corinne asks about the process. The boys uniformly condemn dead stretching, then go on to argue the pluses and minuses of dermal punches, of tapering; they describe for her the steps, they say words like *fistula* as if they are saying elbow or toe, they say "flesh tunnel" and "hypertrophic scars," they know so much and so little. She ekes out the last of the gin.

"We're aiming for the lowest dosage with the highest benefit," Dr. Mosier explained. "Isn't more better?" she asked. She likes flirting with him; she probably should've picked a female shrink. "Not in this case," he said, in his stern psychiatrist voice. But more has always been better! Except, she thinks, when it has been catastrophic.

Poor ears. The boys look ridiculous. They've wrecked themselves for the sake of fashion. She almost removes her shoes to show off the damage high-heels have wrought. They could swap war stories, inventory their wounds, compare scar tissue. She could show them what's what.

At least she didn't say *that* out loud.

"You want another?" the dark-haired boy asks his friend. They order another.

One at this time of day is enough, Corinne thinks. The truth is she never drinks at this time of day. And one drink is never enough. Like great sex without the orgasm: fun, sure, but . . . so sad! No delicious dropping away, no crossing to the other side. She likes it over there. "Take care," she says, sliding off her stool, gathering her things, the daikon, ugly white root, poking obscenely from the eco-bag. The boys give her a low casual wave. She leaves a five-dollar bill on the bar, fighting the bad-tipper stereotype of her demographic.

Perhaps Dr. M. is right. Making decisions that keep her on track—one small decision at a time—will help. There! One drink! Aren't you proud of yourself?

She wants the boys to be watching her, but when she gets to the door and glances back, they are deep in conversation. She feels her phantom nature. At the gym, if she steps off the elliptical to get a drink of water, she returns to a plaintive message on the display screen: ARE YOU THERE?

She should spend next weekend with Gary and Bruce, or visit Sophie, her daughter, up in Seattle. She should reconnect with the friends whose invitations she's refused one too many times in the last six months. Have a dinner party, apologize to everyone, rejoin the human race. She should spend the afternoon going through the files from work, do the tedious fact-checking she's put off, answer the panicky emails from her graphic designer. She should quit this waiting around. She could hear Olivia: "He's not going to call, Corinne. For Christ's sake. Get a life." Get a life. Gimme a break. No big deal. Olivia's catch phrases.

Corinne meanders through the closing market. Vendors dismantle booths, collapse canopies, load crates into hatchback cars and pickups. She needs to get home. She needs to get these flowers in some water. She has already planned dinner, and wonders if she should make it anyway—grilled snapper, fresh peas, Panna Cotta and strawberries for dessert.

Maybe he would still come. Possibly. He said tonight was a good bet. He called her at work yesterday. He said—

Well. She should know better.

Corinne keeps clean men's undershirts in her top drawer. When he's in the bathroom, she exchanges the shirt he was wearing with a fresh one. He never notices. After he leaves, she sleeps in the unwashed shirt, the neckline pulled up over her nose so she can breathe him in. "That's how bad it is," she laughs. She puts her finger to her lips. *Public nuisance*. She checks her phone, then puts it to her ear. "That's how bad it is," she repeats into the phone. "Sometimes," she confides, making her way back to the bookstore where her car is parked, "sometimes, after a particularly rousing round, I have these little red dots on my face—what are those dots?" She pauses as if she's getting an answer, though the phone might as well be a banana or a shoe, held to her ear. "Olivia used to get those. Back when she was throwing up every meal. Her cheeks and nose were speckled with red dots. Broken capillaries? I should google it." So stupid, all that puking, all that drama. Well, she got the last word, didn't she. Yes, she meant business all right. The hose in the exhaust pipe and the garage door closed and a bottle of vodka *and* pills, that was no cry for help, no sirree. She wasn't much older than those loopy-eared boys.

And no note. She and her mother had looked, of course. They searched for days. Nothing.

Corinne nods her head, pretends the person on the other end has said something wise and necessary, as if such a thing exists. She has made her way back to her car. She stands under the bookstore awning, wanting shade, dizzy from sun and gin.

The phone chirps and vibrates against her ear.

"I've got a text," she says. "Tell everyone there hi."

Corinne reads the message, twice. She turns to her reflection in the bookstore window. Yup. Still there. She drops the phone in her bag.

Across the street a woman steps off the curb, into the

crosswalk. She is very precisely in the very middle of the crosswalk. Nonetheless, the car that races past Corinne and into the intersection does not stop. Does not even slow down. The woman can't move out of the way in time. Corinne can't call out in time.

And now the day veers wildly in this other direction. The light shifts, the air is charged. The woman bounces off the hood of the car (a black Toyota) and gains a surprising, almost comical amount of lift, suspended against blue sky before tumbling to asphalt. Corinne runs into the street. She already can't remember when the screech of brakes occurred in relation to the thud of the body, or whether the body itself went over the top of the car or off to the side—she is the closest eyewitness, but the details have been wiped from her mind. The gauge-boys—the handsome one was driving— spring out of the car. Corinne is somehow not surprised to see them. She kneels next to the woman, whose feet are bare, shoes flung who knows where. The knit cap boy yells into his phone, looking at storefronts and street signs, crying out his location. The handsome boy is crying too, oh my God lady are you all right, are you all right?

The woman in the street keeps her eyes on Corinne. *You again!* the gaze seems to say. Corinne meets it. She holds the soft manicured hand, one of the thumbnails now torn. She presses the hand gently. She thinks fleetingly of the week's appointments, dental hygienist and Clinique counter lady and mammogram technician, women scrubbing her gums and moisturizing her face and pressing breasts between glass, each tender touch on chin, neck, shoulder almost making her weep.

She doesn't see any blood but knows not to let the woman move. Her legs are akimbo—a fanciful word for such an awful position. She's in shock, clearly that's what this is. The polka dot skirt is hiked up. Corinne gently adjusts it, so the woman's pale thighs aren't exposed. The contents of her purse lie scattered, lipstick, the signed book of poems, a small stapled pharmacy bag. People gather on the sidewalk but keep their distance, hands on mouths. A siren sounds. That was quick, Corinne thinks, but she has no idea how much time has gone by.

She feels, stupidly, that the accident is her fault. She's the link, the out-of-kilter electrical charge that ignited this chain of events. The dark-haired boy kneels next to her, emitting an acrid smell. Now they will know trouble, these boys. They will know more regret than they deserve.

The woman's eyes begin to lose focus, the light leaking away. She is like a wounded dog, waiting and trusting. She might make it, if she can just hang on. A voice speaks, calm and clear, and for a moment Corinne thinks that the woman is talking to her, reassuring her, and not the other way around. She listens closely and tries to believe what she hears. Hold on, the voice says. Help is on the way.

This Day

My brother died. How did he? He died sick. He died in a hospital room. He died of cancer. He died of pneumonia. He drowned. He couldn't breathe. He died stoned. He died stoned on morphine, more and more morphine, more morphine because he couldn't breathe and he was dying now. I was there. I was holding his feet. Everyone was holding something and I was holding his feet. The bloated yellow feet of a drowning man. He had an IV, tubes, the usual. He had an IV dripping into his body and he was puffed up now. He was big. He almost looked like himself but he didn't. They put the IV in when he went to the hospital. He had to go to the hospital. He was at home and he couldn't breathe. They'd been draining his lungs but now that wasn't enough. He was in his recliner, the La-Z-Boy he had to buy because he couldn't sleep lying down anymore, his back, his bones, so he sat in the recliner most days listening to Crash Test Dummies and the old Jethro Tull albums that used to come through my bedroom wall, back a long time ago, back when we were in the same house, back when we were. He sat in the recliner. I visited him there once. With my new husband and my new baby and he was sitting there. He watched stockcar racing. He watched The Weather Channel. He drank vanilla Ensure. He sat in the recliner and then the day came, months later, when he couldn't breathe, and even then, even after all the carrot juice and green tea and powdered shark cartilage and chemo and the bone marrow transplant that he didn't end up having after all and the almonds and the antineoplastons and the oxygen therapy that he looked into but didn't end up having after all and the macrobiotic diet and the acupuncture and the garlic and the vitamin C, even then he said, I can't believe this is happening.

He had to go to the hospital again. He hated it there. He had to take the ambulance this time because he couldn't breathe. They called me. You have to come now, they said. You have to take the next plane. I took the next plane and I went to the hospital where my brother was asleep. He slept. He kept sleeping. I sat with him while he slept, a coma maybe, maybe a partial coma they said, or maybe the morphine. Sometimes he smiled. I talked to him and held his hands and his feet and tried to get him to say that one last thing that you always want the person to say even though I knew the last time I had seen him had been the real last time and that time I had gone up to his bedroom to tell him I was leaving. I had to go back home. It was time for me to go. He had gotten up from his recliner and gone upstairs to try to sleep. He was very tired that time. I was afraid to go into his room. I was afraid to wake him up. But I was leaving, and he was so sick. In his bedroom piles of clothes, dirty clothes and the sheet on the mattress on the floor where my sick brother lay, that sheet needed changing, that gray sheet needed changing but his wife wouldn't do it, she wouldn't come home on time or remember to bring him food but instead did things like, two hundred dollars for a Juiceman so she could make a fuss about the juice she made him and the Essiac tea she brewed a special complicated way of brewing and the chat rooms where she was finding out about everything. My brother in his grungy bed, and I knew when I said bye, and I knew when he said, Take it easy, he always says take it easy, I knew as I turned down the dark hallway with the clumps of dog hair in the corners and the wind coming through cracked storm windows and the grime on the windowsills like a mold, like something growing there, I knew.

Now it's the next time. Now it's the hospital again. Now it's time. His hands pulling at the sheets, at the tubes. I've seen this before. This is a thing dying people do and I've seen dying people do this before, pulling on the tubes and their clothes, they want everything out and off, they want to get out of here, they can't wait. Get rid of it all the feet and the hands and the skin and the toenails and the hair and the eyebrows and the ears and the voices and they do this strange thing with their hands, they pluck and pull and gather the sheets with their fingers, their fingers won't stop working at the sheets like knitting, like kneading the blankets with their fingers, a nervous picking, they can't stop it, I've seen this before. My brother is doing this. My brother is bunching the sheet in his hands and tugging and pushing the gown away and the catheter the catheter in his penis my brother's brown and withered penis he wants that tube out. He wants that tube out. It is bothering him that tube in his penis. We put the gown back, my weeping mother and I put the sheet back over him. My mother says, Soon, honey. We'll take it out soon. My brother is dying and the tubes will be gone soon. We are one of those families now who have to decide when. We have to let the wife decide. Legally she is the person who decides. She is the wife and she decides. She decides when. We wait until she decides. She is in the cafeteria. She is buying coffee for people she will never see again. We hold his hands to stop their strange knitting and wait while she decides. Then she decides and we are in the room with my brother who is dying. He really is dying now. He really is going to die now. I

am holding his feet. My brother dies and my brother dies
and my brother dies. Who knows while he dies how loud we
are, we can't hear anything, only his silent dying, was that a
breath, was that a last breath, is he still dying or is he dead
now? I am holding his feet. I am holding his feet and my
divorced parents together now for this, for this they are
together they are the mother and father and they are at each
side and the wife is at his head and me the sister the only
sister the only child now the only child I am at his feet. I am
holding his feet. I am just holding his feet. Now my brother
has died. My brother has died now what do we do. Now
what do we do. The wife wants time alone. She is the wife
and she can have that, that time alone, that is all right we all
feel she can have that and we are in the hall and we are doing
what you do when someone dies we are wandering lost in
the land where someone has just died. Other people are there.
This is the ICU. Other people are visiting people in the ICU
and their people have not died yet. Maybe their people won't
die. Their people are hooked up and the machines are still
doing their respirating and stabilizing and circulating and we
are in the land of the dead and they can see us, those other
people, from far away on the other side of the hall and they
are afraid. They watch me, a group of these still-hopeful
people watch me as I hold the pay phone receiver and don't
even have to say it don't even have to say my brother died.
Just call. And the people watching me pretending to move
down the hall but they are not moving, they are standing
there, they can't help it they are staring at me while my
husband talks to me on the phone talks flights, funeral and
those hallway people those ICU people they know where I
am and they are afraid of me, afraid it is their turn next on
that phone. I hang up and find everyone. We have our turns.
We have our turns alone. We have our turns sitting in the
room. Nothing else happens. Nothing else really happens. I
sit in the room. I sit with him. His mouth is open he died

with it open so it is still open and his hair, his hair needs washing, and his feet covered with the sheet now. This is my brother now. This is the end of the story now. This is the end because after that we step into elevators and parking lots and into cars, into the cars we drove here before, into bright June, we drove the cars and parked them here and we knew it was today. It is so bright and I find my sunglasses in my bag but I have ruined them somehow, an emery board in my purse and now my sunglasses have tiny scratches and I can't see out of my sunglasses and I can't see, there are blurry patches over both eyes now. I get into the car where we parked it before, we drove here before and parked the car here and we knew then, we knew we were driving here and we were crossing into something and it would always be this day. It would always be this day. This day would always be. The day we drove our cars here and went to be with my brother because my brother was dying. He died. My brother died. He did die. I was there.

Where Are They Now?

This one was a chemist. Now he's a salesperson for a company that manufactures isotopes. I don't know what this means. I don't know what you use isotopes for or how you make them or who buys them, and if I had married this one, which we talked about doing (though we were very young), then I would have had to memorize a stock bit about isotopes so I could describe his job to other people when they asked. My answer would've had this rehearsed quality to it, and he would've punished me for my indifference.

We lived in a tiny apartment while he was in graduate school. I worked in an athletic wear store at the mall. I had to wear a black and white striped shirt, and a whistle around my neck. This one taught me how to say *spectroscopy* and the formula for converting Fahrenheit into Celsius, which I have forgotten now. Because I didn't already know these things, this one thought I was stupid. He taught me the four fields of energy— electromagnetic field, nuclear strong and weak, and I always forget the other one—and how to hold very still during sex.

This one was recently divorced. His ex-wife had custody of their four children. He was a welder who made enormous metal sculptures. I'm ashamed to think of the things I did or would have done or would do for this one. We lasted for maybe a year, give or take. He was seeing other women all the time we were together. This was the arrangement. These were the rules. Because we lived in a small town, I saw this one with other women at bars, walking in the park, playing Frisbee, drinking coffee, doing the things that we did together when it was my turn to be with him. At that time I was working at a used bookstore. This one bought a book by Grace Paley. That's what got us started, his scarred and callused hands holding *Enormous Changes at the Last Minute*.

This one was, technically, my first. We went to a concert, then back to my dorm room with its narrow twin bed and too many posters on the walls. He was not a student at my college but someone from somewhere else that I had met before. I didn't tell him it was my first time.

This one was a dental lab technician. I was living in Rhode Island, working in a dental lab. I was the waxer. That was my title: "waxer." I had my own Bunsen burner, and my pot of green wax, and I made molds of partial dentures and bridgework and crowns on plaster casts of people's teeth. It took me two months to learn this job, though I only kept it for six. The lab was set up with long tables, each person with his or her own workstation. I sat all day on a tall metal stool. This one sat across from me. He took the molds I made and turned them into metal and honed them down. After work we went drinking. We ate at a clam bar that looked onto the harbor. This one was uncircumcised. He quit the dental lab to drive a truck. He didn't give notice, just left one day. Then he came back. He took me to the truck company and showed me his truck, and the place in the cab where he slept. I thought about leaving with him, traveling down the interstate, up and down the coast. It seemed better than the dental lab. But I didn't go. I slept with this one when I was supposed to be in a monogamous relationship with the future isotope salesman, who was living in a different town at the time.

I was married to this one for nine years.

This one breeds racehorses. He came from money, California money. His father owned racehorse farms in Ireland and Kentucky. I was pretty but not pretty enough for him. He wanted blonde, bikini, like that. We were twenty. We were in college together. I went to four different colleges and this was college number three. We used amphetamines sometimes or cocaine and also birth control but one time, it didn't work. "I have three diaphragm babies at home," the nurse at the clinic told me. I was sick all the time. I walked through the redwood forest that was our campus, thinking about babies. I could move up into a cabin in the mountains, I could join a commune, I could get a job at a coffee shop downtown, the one that was later destroyed in an earthquake. I knew a single mother from my Psychology of Sex Roles class named Rain, and figured she might be of some help. Rain had long stringy hair and carried psychedelic mushrooms in a sandwich baggie in her backpack. Another week went by. I didn't end up talking to Rain.

The doctor had a strange Dutch-sounding name. The doctor hurt me, in spite of the valium and the nurse with the three babies at home holding my hand, and I cried because he was hurting me. "Sometimes life is hard, Janie," he told me. While I was in the room with the Dutch doctor, this one waited for me in the reception area, studying for an economics test. He used a blue highlighter to mark important passages. After that day, he suggested we "take a break." The term ended and I went home for the summer. I transferred to a different school. Later this one wrote me a letter. He had seen *The End of the Road*, he said, and he was sorry.

This one is a rancher. I lived with him on his Montana ranch. I started out young and by the time I left, not so much. I had a job in town at the Kinko's, and other jobs too, all of them the kind I could walk away from at any given moment. This one still lives there, on the ranch, with another woman, a woman with a child, though he told me many times he did not want children.

This one sold vacuum cleaners door to door. I worked in the front office. This one thought he was inventive in bed because he liked to do things with honey and whipped cream. He used to rig sales contests, drawing up false contracts to make it look like our branch had the best sales record in the region. He invented customer names and addresses, thinking he could unload the machines later and cover his tracks, but he usually ended up buying the stuff himself. He won trips to Las Vegas and Palm Beach because of all the phony sales. His wife accompanied him on these trips. This one owned twenty-seven vacuum cleaners and eleven rug shampooers. He eventually went into real estate, of course.

This one looked like Tony Danza but couldn't get it up. So I don't know if he really counts. He worked in a carpet and tile store. We only had the one failed night.

This one I never slept with. He took me out on dates, something I wasn't used to. He would say things like, "I'm co-dependent, big time." He liked Thai food. He ate with his fork in his fist, and his elbow up in the air, parallel to the table. His elbow just stuck way out like that. If someone had been sitting next to him, this one would have jabbed that other person in the ear. When he chewed he neglected to close his mouth. I really couldn't see myself sleeping with someone who ate like that. However, when this one called (I was involved with the welder at the time, but sporadically), he was always solicitous. The nice thing about this one was, he could hear in my voice when I was having a hard time. He could hear me sitting on my kitchen floor, the lights out, the phone cord stretched tight.

Sometimes I stayed very quiet while he talked to me. I sat and listened to his voice, the words spoken slowly, coming from his apartment across town, or one time from a bedroom in his sister's house during a family birthday party. I could hear his nieces and nephews calling out to each other, a grandmother or somebody announcing it was time for cake. This one had been through anger management, divorce, therapy, custody proceedings, AA. He had been in construction but injured his back, so he was getting a degree in social work. This one kept trying but didn't push too hard. This one was a nice man, probably too nice for you, my mother said.

This one is now a reporter, though when we were together, he wanted to be a novelist. We weren't ever really *together*. He drove us to the beach one day. We drank a bottle of wine and on the way back to the car, he peed in the bushes, but I was much younger than he was, and too self-conscious to pee in the bushes. Now I'd pee in the bushes, or make him stop at a gas station. I had to pee so badly all the way to his house, I couldn't speak. He was renting a farmhouse by the ocean and writing his novel. We ate dinner there that night, and I stayed with him. Afterwards he asked me if it was my first time. He wanted me to be a virgin, so I said yes. The next morning we went to the grocery store. I checked the eggs in the carton to make sure none were broken or stuck, wiggling each egg. "Why are you counting the eggs?" he asked me. Now every time I buy eggs, touching each one first, I think of this one, though it is thirty years later and he probably doesn't even remember me or else he remembers me, but not the eggs, not at all.

This one had just gotten off Methadone. He had a silver tooth and a small gold hoop in his ear. He worked in a factory that made pencils. He smelled of wood chips and lead. This one played bass in a jazz band. I was working as a waitress then. He lived near a lake and used to throw things into the water while we talked—pebbles, sticks. He liked to talk about how heroin was better than sex. He was especially fond of oral sex. He had an ex-wife named Crystal and many grudges against those who had not given him a fair shake in the music business. When I quit my job and left town, he wanted to come with me. I didn't think this was such a great idea. *Smoldering anger* is the phrase that comes to mind. I packed up my car early one morning, before it was light, my tip money spilled onto the front seat for tolls and gas. I don't know where this one is now.

This one was a girl. I liked kissing her but the other stuff made me nervous. We watched *Dallas* reruns and fooled around on her couch until her lover came home and started throwing things—refrigerator magnets, trivets, an ashtray. This one lives in Minnesota, does massage therapy; she calls now and then, promises to come see me.

This one's dog was named *Garçon*. I loved that dog. This one married his high school sweetheart. He worked at a bank in Boston, ran three marathons a year, and died at forty-five years old. According to his obituary, this one left behind seven children.

This one was from boarding school. He played Jean-Pierre Rampal records and taught me to say "flautist." His father was a history professor, married to a much younger woman. His mother lived with a toy inventor. She told me that when they moved into their loft, the previous owner had left behind a black dildo. She waited for me to be shocked, but I was fifteen, naive—I didn't know what a dildo was.

I was in love and wanted to lose my virginity to this one, but he said no.

After formal dinner one night, he said we needed to talk. Still, even when he said *we need to talk*, I didn't see it coming. I didn't have any idea about anything. I was wearing a denim dress with big square pockets on the front and a square neckline, a pearl ring on my right hand, and a silver barrette in my hair. We walked to the library, which was one of our favorite places to make out. We sat at the back table. I read the words people had carved into the wood, words I had read many times before. "What a long, strange trip it's been." "I am a rock, I am an island." "Fuck you."

He didn't love me, he said. He loved someone else. They were sleeping together. She meant everything to him. He was sorry.

I went back to my room. I sat on my bed, my hands in the big pockets. I guess I was there a long time. Finally someone went to get the R.A.

Danielle Hamilton was the name of his new girl. She was a day student, with parents who left her home alone most weekends.

Recently I saw this one at a class reunion. A group of us had drinks at the hotel, everyone older of course, some of the men almost unrecognizable without their hair, but then they would speak and their voices were exactly the same. If you closed your eyes, you were fifteen again, drinking beer in the parking lot behind the Commons.

This one sat next to me. The subject at our table was love. We were all either divorced or on second and third marriages. But we had been young together, and a nostalgic mood was, after all, the point of the weekend. So this one talked about Danielle.

"I've never felt that way before or since. She was the love of my life."

"I know," I reminded him, "you broke up with me, to be with her."

He was puzzled. "No I didn't, Janie." I could see him trying to sort it out in his head, like calculating how much tip to leave, or recalling the lyrics to a song you once knew.

No I didn't. This one didn't remember breaking my heart! I wondered if he remembered being with me at all. I started to laugh, and, truth be told, once I got going, it was difficult to stop.

SUSAN JACKSON RODGERS grew up in Connecticut and New York City. She earned her B.A. from Bowdoin College, her M.A. from Kansas State University, and her M.F.A. from Bennington College. She is the author of *The Trouble With You Is and Other Stories* (Mid-List Press, 2004). She lives in Corvallis, Oregon with her husband and three children, and teaches at Oregon State University. Her website is www.susanjacksonrodgers.com.

Cover artist **COLBY JOHNSON** first decided to take pictures while in Big Cottonwood Canyon, wanting to be able to show others the magnificent sites he was seeing while hiking. He borrowed his first camera from his dad and after realizing how much he enjoyed taking pictures he purchased his own. After taking thousands of pictures with his camera and honing his skills, he decided to start selling fine art prints with his brother, Cliff.

Colby can be contacted at colby@lazydayphoto.com. Visit his website at www.lazydayphoto.com and see more of his work on Flickr at http://www.flickr.com/photos/theubersquid/

From the Author

Warm thanks to Kevin Morgan Watson at Press 53 for his enthusiastic embracing of this manuscript, which came at just the right time. His unflagging support of short story writers and poets is rare these days, and a great gift. Christine Norris offered excellent editorial suggestions and corrections. Collaborating on the cover design with Nancy Froehlich and her class of typography students at Oregon State University was a pleasure.

Some of these stories were written while I worked on my later-in-life MFA degree at Bennington College, and I want to thank my writing teachers for their guidance, and my fellow students for support and good times. Thanks, too, to longtime and cherished friends in Manhattan, Kansas—too many to name. Paula Ford, I will miss you always.

I am daily appreciative of the community I have found in my new academic home. Special thanks to Tracy Daugherty, Anita Helle, Karen Holmberg, and Keith Scribner, and to my dear pal Marjorie Sandor. The OSU Center for the Humanities has given me much valued space and time to work.

Love and gratitude to my mother, Maggie Jackson. Her talents as an actress and director, as well as my late father's filmmaker's eye, have informed and enriched my creative life immeasurably.

Sam, Meg, and Ben: Where did you amazing people come from? No, seriously—how did I get so lucky? You are my joy, love, pride, delight. I can't imagine better.

And gratitude, above all, to my husband, Larry. Without whom...

CPSIA information can be obtained at www.ICGtesting.com
Printed in the USA
LVOW122054150313

324403LV00004B/13/P